Sea Wrack and Changewind
All of the Archers Beach Short Stories
Sharon Lee

Table of Contents

Copyright Page

"Emancipated Child" originally appeared on Splinter Universe July 2012, "How Nathan Archer Came to be a Prince of the Land of the Flowers" originally appeared on Splinter Universe, September 2012, "The Gift of Music" originally appeared on Baen.com, January 2014, "The night don't seem so lonely" originally appeared on Baen.com January 2015, "Will-o'-the-Wisp" originally appeared on Splinter Universe January 2016, "The Wolf 's Bride" originally appeared on Splinter Universe January 2016, "The Road to Pomona's" originally appeared on Splinter Universe October 2016, "The Vestals of Midnight" originally appeared in Release the Virgins, edited by Michael A. Ventrella, Gray Rabbit Publications, January 2019, "Wolf in the Wind" originally appeared in part on Splinter Universe August 2023. "About this Book," is original to this volume.

Pinbeam Books
PO Box 1586
Waterville ME 04903
email: info@pinbeambooks.com
ISBN: 978-1-948465-29-8
Cover art: SelfPubBookCovers.com/Daniela_93839
Published by Pinbeam Books December 2024

Many thanks to Bex O for deploying her tyop hunting skills on behalf of this book.

About this Book

The first thing you need to know is that I am a child of the ocean. I never feel so alive as when I'm at the beach, with the waves crashing at my feet, a damp breeze slapping my cheeks, and the smell of salt clogging my nose.

The sea – by which I mean the Atlantic Ocean – has always been, to me, a place of infinite possibility, sitting on the border between the everyday and the magical. I've never lived at the ocean – though not for lack of trying – but I've never in my life lived more than 60 miles from salt water. One of the conditions that I made when Steve and I were deciding to move from Maryland to New England, back in 1989, was that we settle at or near the ocean.

The second thing you need to know is that I love amusement parks, and I *adore* carousels. I know, I know. Round and round, up and down, caught in an endless web of three-fourths time – not exactly the stuff of heroes.

And yet, circles are deeply magical – ask any wizard at his spelling. The sun, the moon, the earth are circles. Life itself is said to be a circle.

Put a carousel at the ocean, and I am *so* there.

Sometime after that move from Maryland to, as it turned out, Maine, I discovered Old Orchard Beach, a no-longer fashionable resort town on that rarity of the Maine coast – seven miles of sand beach. OOB quickly became a favorite destination. We vacationed there on those occasions when we could afford a vacation. When we couldn't afford to stay, well – it was a quick drive south for an hour or a day at the beach, and we made that trip as often as we could.

All that said, and in the way of writers, one day I turned to Steve and said, "I ought to write a book about this place."

Which I did. In fact, I wrote three books about Archers Beach, Maine, an aging resort town where magic and mundane meet – *Carousel Tides*, *Carousel Sun*, *Carousel Seas*, published by Baen in 2010, 2014, and 2015.

In the way of such things, the novels spawned short stories, which were collected now and again, in chapbooks from Pinbeam Books, the Sharon Lee and Steve Miller indie publishing arm.

Eventually, in response to reader input, queries were made, and Tantor agreed to produce an audiobook of the Archers Beach shorts, if they were all collected into one place.

And that's what this is: All of the Archers Beach short stories, conveniently collected in one place; a companion volume for the upcoming audiobook.

Enjoy the stories.

Thank you.

Sharon Lee
Cat Farm and Confusion Factory
December 2024

Emancipated Child

Jason's lungs were on fire, and he could hear Matt's sneakers pounding on the trail behind him over the harsh rasp of his breath. Matt was taller than he was, and on the track team, but Jason had a head start.

"Too good for us, you little bastard? I'll show you too good!" It was worrisome that Matt had breath left over from running to yell with. Jason couldn't have answered if he wanted to, which he didn't. All he wanted to do was to get the hell gone, out of Matt's range—which wasn't going to happen, so the next best thing was to get to the store, where there would be people—or at least Johnna. Not even Matt was stupid enough to beat somebody up in front of a witness.

On the right he saw the shortcut that took a corner off the main trail and would put him in the store's parking lot in a couple of minutes.

Assuming Matt didn't catch him first.

Jason took the turn into the shortcut hard, sand and pebbles skidding underfoot. He took a hard breath and felt it come easier, deeper, even as his short legs found a renewed burst of speed. Second wind, he thought, pelting down the thin trail between high walls of cattail and swamp grass. He could still hear Matt behind him, but it sounded like his cousin hadn't found his own second wind.

In fact, it sounded like he was laboring, his pursuing footsteps not pounding so much as . . . sliding; almost as if the sand were loose, rather than packed down hard.

Jason ran on, fists pumping, breathing hard, but not gasping, suddenly feeling as if he could keep on running forever. He took a curve in the path at speed, dodging the skinny dead tree that made the way even thinner.

Must be that runner's high the jocks talked about. Jason flew on.

"Hey!" Matt yelled from behind him, surprise sounding amidst a loud crack and a clatter like sticks being flung onto stone. "Hey, ow!"

Ow?

Jason slowed, and dared to look back over his shoulder. Matt might be going to kill him, but they were cousins, and if he was really hurt—

He got one glimpse of the old tree, now missing the limb that had overhung the path, and Matt pushing himself to his knees. If that limb had hit—

This way!

His sleeve was snatched and he was yanked to the right, through a tangle of dry reeds and out again into a small grassy place, hemmed in with ash and marsh willow.

Jason staggered to a stop, feeling damp and exhausted. Before him, a grey stone thrust out of the grass. Jason collapsed onto its conveniently flat top as if it were a stool, closed his eyes and waited for his heart-rate to come down. He strained his ears, but he didn't hear any signs of pursuit, which made him wonder again if his cousin was hurt.

And how much he cared.

"I've got to get to work pretty soon," he said out loud to the glade in general.

There was no response, unless you counted the sudden whistle of a red-winged blackbird. He hadn't really expected a response, but he did try to be polite. His dad, back before the cancer, had said that it was the least a man who heard voices could do, was to be polite.

The voices themselves—well. He'd heard them his whole life, sometimes direct, like the one that had yelled at him to get off the trail this way. Mostly, though, they were a comfortable background noise. The voices were company, sort of, like a radio playing somewhere in the house made you feel less alone.

"Why does he hate you?" a rough voice asked then—an out loud voice, not at all like the voices in his head, and one Jason had never heard before.

He turned his head, carefully.

A girl was leaning against a swamp maple, arms crossed over her chest. She might've been his age, her face was brown, and her hair, too. She was wearing a bottle green t-shirt and brown cargo pants. Her eyes were the same green as her t-shirt.

Not somebody he knew, and he knew everybody in Surfside. 'Course, there wasn't any law said she couldn't've come across the walking path higher up in the main marsh; or down, from Scarborough; or up, from Archers Beach.

"Well," Jason said carefully. "He doesn't really *hate* me so much as he's pretty mad at me."

The girl's eyebrows lifted.

"Why is he pretty mad, then?"

None of your business, was on the tip of his tongue, but . . . he had a . . . *feeling.*

Besides, it wasn't like it was a state secret.

"He's mad 'cause I'm emancipated," he said. "His folks and him figure that means I think I'm too good for them."

"What is emancipated?" she asked, which he could've predicted for the next question. *Everybody* asked that one.

"It means I petitioned the court to be able to—to leave my parent's authority and house, and to live on my own." The full legal name was *emancipated child*, which he didn't bother to say, because he was, ferchristsake, *not* a child. He was sixteen, and fully in control of his own life.

He took a breath and answered the next most common question before she could ask it.

"And the reason I did it is because my dad died and my mom . . . She moved out of town, up to Portland, and in with—"

. . . *with her coke-head boyfriend*. He swallowed that. There was such a thing as *too* personal, after all.

". . .with a friend. We don't get along—me and the friend—and besides I didn't want to live in Portland." He'd been sick in Portland; all the time—not bad sick, like cancer, or anything like that. Just that his head hurt, and his stomach was queasy, kinda, and he hadn't been able to hear the voices in his head over all the rush and racket.

He took another breath. "So I got a job doing handywork at the Sunspray, and I showed I was able to be independent and all."

"And that boy is angry because you are emancipated and he is not?"

Jason laughed. "No—oh, *hell* no! Matt's hot—well, I'm guessing he caught it from his mom—she's my mom's sister. They just all figured I should move in with them, see? Except that wasn't going to work, either." Because him and Matt weren't exactly best friends even when he wasn't channeling Aunt Dottie's anger—and her taste in boyfriends wasn't any better than *his* mom's, and besides that—they lived in Scarborough.

No reason to say any of that, either, to some strange girl chance-met in the marsh, so he shifted on the rock and said instead, "I'm gonna hafta get to work pretty soon."

"So that you remain emancipated." She nodded and pushed away from the tree she'd been leaning against. "I'll walk with you," she said, "to Johnna's store."

"Sure," he said, sliding off the rock.

She was taller than he was, which almost everybody was, so no surprises there; and skinny in a way that said she might've just had a growth spurt.

"I'm Jason Thibodeau," he said, as she stepped in front of him and disappeared into the wall of reeds. "By the way."

He followed her, holding an arm in front of his eyes, but it—it almost seemed like the reeds bent out of his way. There must, he told himself, be a trail—maybe a deer track—that the girl knew about and that he just didn't see.

She was waiting for him on the path, looking back the way he had come. He snuck a look that way, himself. The dead tree stood where it always had, one of its limbs down and shattered across the path.

There wasn't any sign of Matt. Jason breathed a sigh of relief.

"Your cousin was not hurt," the girl said. "Only frightened."

"That's good," he said, and added, "though I can't think of much that would scare Matt."

She snorted lightly, maybe it was a laugh, and turned toward Johnna's store, walking to the left of the path and slightly ahead of him.

"What's your name?" Jason asked, after they'd gone a couple dozen steps in silence.

She glanced at him over her shoulder—a flash of green eyes behind rough brown hair.

"Cedar," she said. "Cedar White."

"You live around here?"

She snorted another laugh. "Oh, yes."

"New?" he asked, which people from Away might think was rude, he remembered, and added a reason for why he might care. "Hadn't seen you in school, is all."

"Ah," she said, and gave him another, slower, look from behind her hair. "I am schooled at home."

That set a tingle up his nerves—a lie if he'd ever heard one. He could tell, usually, when people were telling the truth. Still, lying about being home-schooled didn't prove she was a run-away—that? Was probably his own nerves talking, since he'd put some thought into what he'd do, and where he'd go, while he was waiting for the court to decide his case, knowing how slim his chances were for a win, and wondering if he had the guts to run away, if he didn't win.

Lucky for him, it hadn't come to that, because where would he have run to, except back to Surfside, year-round population just six souls under 200, and no place at all to hide?

The path widened into a dirt parking lot. Jason stretched his legs so he was walking beside Cedar and then had to drop back again when she mounted the step onto the porch, opened the door, stepped inside—and paused, the door balanced on brown fingertips.

He grabbed it hurriedly. "Thanks."

Johnna was working in the front of the middle cooler—making sure the beer was stocked and cold for the home-coming crew, Jason knew. She looked 'round when the bell rang and straightened.

"You want something?" she asked, glaring at Cedar.

The girl nodded. "Work."

"An' you figure *I* got work?" Johnna shook her head and looked over Cedar's shoulder to Jason.

"Cousin of yours was in here, says to let you know, if you should happen by, that he'll see you in school tomorrow."

"Thanks." He slipped past Cedar, opened up the front cooler, pulled out a can of root beer and a pre-made ham sandwich on white bread.

"That all you havin' for supper, boy?" Johnna asked him, like she did every day.

He shook his head, like he did every day. "Just to get me through work," he said. "I'll have supper when I get home."

"You see you do. Vegetables, I'm talking."

"Carrots," he promised her, fishing a couple dollar bills out of his jeans pocket. He put them on the counter by the register, then looked to the girl, standing silent to one side.

"You need something to eat?" he asked her. "It's on me."

She blinked green eyes at him, the side of her mouth turning up like she'd tasted something bad.

"You never mind 'bout her," Johnna said, letting the door to the cooler thump shut. "Dinner comes with the shift." She gave Cedar another glare, not exactly, Jason thought, friendly, before she turned it on him.

"You'd best get on 'fore Vonny dings you for being late."

Jason sighed and gathered up his soda and sandwich. While he'd been lucky to get the job at the Sunspray, there wasn't any sense in pretending that Bob Varney, his boss, was anything but a mean sonofabitch. He'd greeted the news of Jason's successful emancipation with a frown and a look in his eye that Jason just knew meant he was thinking about how much grief and trouble he could cause, if he turned the kid off, since staying employed was one of the major terms of his independence. If Jason lost his job, he was supposed to report himself to the Department of Health and Human Services, so he could be placed in a foster home.

Like he was *that* dumb.

"I'm going," he told Johnna, and gave Cedar a nod.

"Thanks," he said to her.

It wasn't until he was across the road and sprinting down the Sunspray's long drive that he wondered what he'd been thanking her for.

. . . .

IT HAD BEEN YARD WORK today—Jason's favorite and the primary reason Mr. Varney'd taken him on. Mr. Varney was an electrician by trade, with some carpentry and plumbing on the side—a true handyman. What he had no feeling or care for was plants and lawns and trees, so all that sort of thing fell to Jason. Since it also kept him out of his boss' way—and under his radar—it was all good as far as Jason was concerned.

Work of the day had been putting down pine chips around the tree trunks, and in the two big gardens at the front of the building.

He put his back into it, enjoying the breeze, the early-spring lack of bugs, the scent of the wood chips, and the easy, familiar murmur of the voices in his head.

When his watch beeped the half-shift warning, he left his tools and the wheelbarrow where they were, grabbed his sandwich and root beer and walked to the back of the building, letting himself out by the beach-gate.

What had been a breeze inside the protected grounds was a wind here on the sand, running toward the shore on the back of the incoming tide. Jason crossed the dunes on the board walkway, and turned right, walking down the beach to the Rock.

The Rock was something of a landmark, and it marked the boundary between Surfside and Archers Beach, the town next door. The Rock had been one of his father's favorite places—maybe his favorite place, in town. Even when he'd barely been able to walk, he'd manage to get to the Rock, and sit down on the sand with his back against it. It made him feel better, he said, to visit with an old friend.

After his dad died, Jason hadn't visited the Rock much—he'd told himself because there'd been too much other stuff going on, but the truth—the *real* truth was that he hadn't forgiven the Rock—

Hadn't forgiven it for not saving his father.

Which was just stupid, little-kid thinking. Like a rock—no matter how old—could keep a man from dying of stomach cancer . . .

He'd made a point of visiting since he'd come back to town, most days eating his half-shift snack with his back companionably braced against the Rock's sea-washed surface. He was pretty sure the Rock understood, and forgave him for being an idiot.

Today, he leaned against the leeward side of the Rock while he ate his sandwich. He balled up the wrapping and stuck it in his pocket, drained his root beer, stuck the empty in his other pocket, and headed back to the Sunspray, feeling peaceable and content.

It wasn't far—nothing in Surfside was very far from anything else; it was only a little strip of land between Archers Beach and Pine Point—a silly little bit of land that nobody wanted, nestled between the marsh and the sea. The Sunspray was the biggest—and newest—thing in Surfside, hardly ten years old. Before the Sunspray, there'd been an old "tourist resort" on the land, built 'way back at the end of World War I. People from Away would take a train up to Archers Beach, then, that's what Johnna'd told him, and some of them would ride the trolley out to the tourist resort.

Now, people from Away drove up in their Infinitis, their BMWs, and their Lexuses, to their condo summer homes, swelling Surfside's population to almost three hundred for the ten or twelve weeks of summer.

There wasn't much to do in Surfside, of course, outside of laying on the beach. The excitement was down in Archers Beach, with its amusement park, and the Pier; the bars and restaurants. If you wanted a beer in Surfside, you bought a six-pack at Johnna's store; if you wanted to eat in a restaurant, you went someplace else.

He was walking briskly; the Sunspray's boardwalk, with its all-weather grey paint and railings on both sides, was just ahead. On his right was the utility shed where the Sunspray kept beach chairs and umbrellas for its residents, the door swinging in the wind off the sea.

Jason frowned. The door was supposed to be padlocked, and Mr. Varney held the key. He guessed one of the hinges could have rusted through, but—

But, no, he saw, as he reached the shed. The padlock was through one metal hasp, but not through both. If Mr. Varney'd been in a hurry, that might explain it, though why he'd be in the shed at this time of year . . .

Jason grabbed the door, automatically pulling it wide, to make sure that the chairs were in place.

They were.

And piled around and on top of them were a number of what looked to be bricks, wrapped in black plastic—and they didn't belong there, at all.

. . . .

"OK, BACK TO WORK," Mr. Varney said, snapping the lock through both hasps and yanking on it hard to make sure it had caught.

"But," Jason said, "what are those things?"

His boss gave him a hard stare.

"Stuff I'm holding for a friend, all right? Be gone in a dayer two. Nothin' to do with you, and nothin' to be blabbing about to Sodeby, neither."

Mr. Sodeby was the site manager. Mr. Varney's boss.

There was probably a policy against Mr. Varney using Sunspray property to store "things" for a friend. On the other hand, Mr. Varney could fire him, and then where would he be?

So—

"Sure," Jason said.

. . . .

NOBODY WAS CHASING him today—nobody had to. Matt had gotten in some good licks right after gym, with the help of Danny Walker, who'd tripped him, and then, when he was getting up, after Matt was done with him, had casually slammed him into the wall.

He'd staggered in after them, heading for the nearest bathroom, and hadn't quite gotten all the blood off his face when the door opened and Mr. Marks, the principal, walked in.

So, on top of a black eye, a wrenched knee, and a very sore stomach, he had Saturday detention.

For fighting on school property.

He stepped from the main trail onto the Surfside trail, limping, and shook his head. Things might've gone a little easier with Mr. Marks, if he'd said who he'd been fighting with, which he hadn't done, not even when the threat of suspension had been brought out. First of all—it was a bogus threat; Mr. Marks would look a right fool for suspending a kid for fighting with himself. Especially an honor-roll kid.

Second—wouldn't Matt just kill him *dead* if he squealed.

So, now he was going to have to negotiate with Mr. Varney for four morning hours off on Saturday, his only full-workday, and right when there was the spring yard work to do. It was staying light now until seven, seven-thirty, so he figured he could pick up a couple of the Saturday hours in the evening—and maybe work late on Friday, too. That was what he'd offer Varney. He rounded the bend in the path with a heartfelt sigh. Almost there; the shortcut was just up ahead—

And there was somebody waiting on the edge of the path. Jason tensed, not recognizing the shadow against the weeds, and knowing for sure he wasn't running any—

The figure turned, stepped full into the path and came toward him.

Jason let his breath out in a rush.

"Cedar White, hey," he said, as nonchalantly as he could. She stopped in the middle of the trail, her hands on her hips, and a frown on her face.

"What happened to you?"

"Well." Since she was blocking the trail, he stopped, too. "My cousin saw me in school today, like he told Johnna to tell me he would."

"And he tried to kill you."

He shook his head. "Just make me sorry." He sighed. "Which I am. Sorry on all fronts, looks like. Got Saturday detention for fighting on school grounds, so I need to convince Mr. Varney to let me work late on Friday and late on Saturday, to make up the time."

He closed his eyes. Opened them. "Which means I've gotta move on, if you don't mind."

She didn't take the hint. "If you accepted your power, these things would not happen to you," she said.

He blinked at her. "Accept my *power*?" He opened his arms wide. "Do I look like somebody who has *power* to you?"

"In fact," she said, suddenly moving to one side of the trail, "you do. You look to me like the Guardian of this Land. Don't you hear it talking to you? Don't you hear *me* talking to you?"

He had started walking again—almost stopped, and satisfied himself with sending her a hard stare.

"I hear *you* talking to me because you're talking to me," he said, and didn't ask, *How do you know about the voices? Do you hear them, too?*

She walked beside him, keeping pace with his limp.

"I could help you more if you accepted the Land," she said, as they crossed the parking lot. "Johnna could, and others of the *trenvay*."

Great. Yesterday, he'd met a girl. She was weird, but who wasn't? Today, she let him know that she was a total nutcase.

No, he thought, painfully, that's not fair. After all, his father hadn't laughed at him when he said he heard voices. His father, who had counted a big old beach rock as one of his longest-held and best friends.

He sighed.

"Do you hear the voices?" he asked her.

Her mouth bent a little. He thought it might've been her version of a smile.

"I'm not the Guardian," she said; "I'm *trenvay*."

She went up the stairs ahead of him, opened the door, stepped through and stood holding it open for him.

"Thanks," he said. And, "What's that, exactly? *Trenvay*?"

"In my case, it means I live in a tree," she said. "Other *trenvay* have other . . . arrangements." Another sharp green stare from behind her hair.

"Didn't your father tell you these things?"

"His father," Johnna said, from behind the counter, "din't more'n half-believe, himself. Not so much gave himself to the Land, as accepted he was a little touched in the head." She nodded at Jason. "It was a bad day when you told him you heard voices. Figured you'd inherited, which you had. Sat here on the floor with his back against the counter, just drinking beer right outta my cooler and crying like a little baby."

"My dad thought I was nuts?" Jason asked. "Just like him?"

"That's it. Should've known better, but his grandma—goin' back now a good number of years, to the buildin' of the old resort—his grandma died early, leaving a baby an' a husband who was deafer'n a barn door. The baby—his ma—she talked about what she heard, but she din't have the lore. Her pa finally took her off to Portland for a cure. She come back . . . broke. Married who he said, then did what *he* said. Had a baby—your dad—then . . . just faded into the wind. I seen *trenvay* go that way, a time or two, but never a mortal creature. Your dad, all he knew was that his ma'd heard things and gotten trouble for it, so he din't ever say, nor ask no questions." She sighed and shook her head.

"We been without a long time, Jason. It'd be good—for the Land, and the *trenvay*—"

"And him," Cedar said, moving to the cooler and pulling out a wrapped ham sandwich and a root beer. She put them on the counter and looked hard at Johnna. "*And him.* Don't forget that."

"Some things'll be easier," said Johnna, looking stubborn. "Other things, won't."

"Sounds like life," Jason said, shaking his head. "Look, unless being—what? Guardian?—is something I can put on my resume and show the DHS if they ask am I employed, I'm going to have to pass, and—" he glanced to the clock on the back wall—"get to work."

He reached into his pocket, and stopped when Johnna waved a hand. "Get on with ya."

"I'll carry," Cedar said, snatching up the root beer and sandwich. "You walk."

• • • •

THEY WERE HALF-WAY up the Sunspray's drive when he asked her, feeling like an idiot.

"So, how would I go about accepting my power, assuming I have any?"

She shook her hair back out of her face and gave him a straight look. Her eyes, he saw—the brilliant, bright green wasn't the oddest thing about them. The oddest thing about them was that they didn't have any whites—they were green, with dark rings.

Not . . . regular . . . human . . . eyes.

"To accept your power, you only need to reach to the Land, and welcome it in," she said.

Right.

"Sounds simple enough. I'll try it one day when I'm bored," he said, mildly.

They were at the maintenance entrance. He turned, painfully, and held out his hands.

"Thanks for carrying. I'll take it from here."

She handed over the sandwich and root beer without a word, and turned away. He used his key in the lock, and pushed the door open, wincing at the protest of his bruises.

When he looked down the drive, Cedar was nowhere to be seen.

• • • •

MR. VARNEY WASN'T IN the office, or in any of his other usual places. Jason sighed, half in relief and half in frustration, clocked in, grabbed his shovel and rake, and went out to the back where the pile of pine bark and the wheelbarrow waited for him.

By the time he'd gotten the chips in the barrow, and the barrow around the side, he was sweating and shivering. Stupid.

He had to do his job. *Had* to. Bad enough to have to talk to Varney about shifting his work hours around the detention. But if it looked like he was slacking off . . .

"Sit down," said a rough, familiar voice, "and tell me what to do."

He looked up into Cedar's not-human green eyes.

"I've got to put the chips around the base of the trees, to keep the weeds down."

"I will do it," she said, taking the shovel out of his hand. "You will sit down on that wall and supervise me."

"I don't—"

"I know," she interrupted, turning to the wheelbarrow, "a very great deal about trees."

• • • •

SHE WAS A WILLING WORKER, and strong, too. He had to get up twice, to show her how to rake the chips into neat, unnatural circles, so that nothing untidy upset the eyes of the Sunspray's residents. She pursed her lips, and he got a feeling like she wasn't exactly pleased with the idea, but she *got* it, and raked.

He watched her, and . . . dozed.

Immediately he closed his eyes, the constant background hum of the voices increased, and he felt a . . . drawing-in, as if friends were coming close around him, to shield him from the wind. He sighed, comforted and . . . safe.

Safe.

Now, wasn't that a peculiar feeling.

"Jason."

He opened his eyes, looking directly into Cedar's face. "What?" he asked, groggily, then panic took him, chasing away the residual feeling of *safe*. "Is Mr. Varney back?"

"I don't know," she answered carelessly. "What I do know is *that* tree is sick." She raised an arm and pointed.

He squinted along the line of her arm to a grey birch. "It looks all right to me."

"It might look all right," she said sharply. "But it's not. You can cure it."

He blinked at her. "No, I can't."

"Yes," she said, the *ess* a positive hiss, "you can. What's more, if you accepted your power, you could cure yourself, too."

He sighed. "Cedar, look. . ."

"Halloo!" came a shout. "Hey, Vonny! Anybody here?" This was followed by the sound of a door being pounded vigorously.

Jason came to his feet, gasping as every single one of his bruises protesting.

"They better knock it off before Mr. Sodeby hears it," he said, hobbling as fast as he could toward the back of the building.

He heard an exasperated sigh, glanced to his side, and wasn't really surprised to see Cedar keeping pace with him.

"What is this to you?"

"If whoever that is doesn't quiet down, he'll draw Mr. Sodeby. Mr. Sodeby will take a chunk out of Mr. Varney, who will then take a chunk out of me. Think trickle-down economics."

They'd reached the side door by this time, just as the man started a renewed assault on the door.

"Can I help you?" Jason called, hobbling as fast as he could. The man turned around—nobody he knew; maybe a lobsterman down from Pine Point, or a clam-digger. He was unshaven without being bearded, his sweater was rough, and his jeans were tough. He was wearing boots, scarred and salt-stained.

"I'm looking for Vonny," he said. "S'pose to meet me."

"I'm Jason Thibodeau," he said; "Mr. Varney's assistant. He's not here right now. Is there something I can help you with?"

"Well, yeah, maybe so." The man jerked his head beachward. "Need the key to that shed o'his."

Jason's heart sank. The key to the shed was on Mr. Varney's personal ring that he always had on him.

"I'm sorry," he said to the man, "I don't have access to the key. If you'd like to wait in the garden, I'll go—" But the man had already turned away.

"Second time that sumbitch ain't here when I come by. Starting to get the feelin' he don't wanna see me. That's all right; I'll take care of it my own self."

He turned away and strode toward the dune-gate.

Jason stared after him. The beach wasn't private, exactly, but the shed—if this guy was going to vandalize the shed—

"Hey!" he yelled, limping after the man.

"Jason, he didn't want your help," Cedar said from beside him.

"Well, but—"

"And—" She pointed across the pool court, to a quick moving shadow. "Is that Mr. Varney?"

It was, Jason saw with relief, and he was moving fast for a big man. He'd left his toolbelt off, but he had a hammer in his hand. The dune-gate slammed behind the loud man. Mr. Varney waited, like he was counting, then eased the gate open just far enough so he could slip through, and kept a hand on it, so it shut again, silently.

Jason bit his lip and kept on, limping across the court with Cedar beside him.

"Why?" she demanded. "It's between them, whatever it is, and has nothing to do with you!"

He shook his head.

"Could be—I don't know, trouble. That guy was pretty mad. Don't want him to get into a fight with Mr. Varney."

"Why not?" asked Cedar, which was a good question, actually. So good that Jason decided to ignore her and shambled into a run. By the time he reached the dune-gate, the boardwalk was empty.

He opened the gate, carefully. Cedar, behind him, sighed loudly, but made sure the gate didn't smack home, and followed him down the walk, and over the dunes.

• • • •

THERE WAS A PICK-UP truck parked on the far side of the umbrella shed, its nose pointed south, toward Archers Beach.

By the shed itself was the loud man, bent over the lock, working at it with—a screwdriver, maybe.

Almost immediately behind him was Mr. Varney, choking the hammer tight and raising it as he stepped forward—

Jason yelled.

The man at the shed dropped the lock and spun, lunging with—

Not a screwdriver, Jason saw—a knife.

He jumped from the end of the boardwalk into the dry sand, and flailed, his wrenched knee buckling. All at once, he found his feet, and ran toward the two men.

Mr. Varney swung down with the hammer, striking the loud man's shoulder. He grunted, but didn't draw back. Mr. Varney swung the hammer again, and this time he connected.

The loud man fell like a tree.

Jason stopped where he was, staring at the scene before him, Mr. Varney holding the hammer, looking down at his fallen opponent, a red stain beginning to show on the side of his work shirt.

The other man . . .

Jason looked down. He wasn't bleeding, not that could be seen, but that had been a hell of a whack Mr. Varney'd—

It came to him, with the force of an irrefutable fact, that the loud man was dead.

"You killed him," he said, his voice flat.

Mr. Varney turned slowly, letting the hammer fall from his hand.

"Him?" he said, walking toward Jason. "Take more'n a tap on the head to kill *him*. This is gonna work out just fine."

He raised his arm. Jason staggered back, trying to twist out of the path of the descending fist—

• • • •

"THAT WORKED WELL," a familiar voice breathed in his ear. "Jason?"

He pried his eyes open against the pounding of his head. "Cedar. Where's—"

"Another man came across the dunes in a buggy," she said, talking fast. "He's helping Mr. Varney unload packages from the shed. Mr. Varney said he would call the cops when the other man was gone, and turn you in for killing Remmy Jule. He said," she swallowed hard, and Jason, looking at her closely, saw that she was crying. "He said that would keep you out of Surfside."

Her face twisted. "Damn you, Jason, why did you have to fall on the beach? The Land can't help you here!"

He stared at her. Keep him out of Surfside? In jail, that would be. For murder. He'd *never* come back home, never hear the voices again . . .

"I accept my power," he whispered, hoarsely.

Cedar shook her head violently. "Idiot! The beach is neutral! You need *to be on* the Land!"

He didn't think he could move, and anyway— "Can they see me? Varney and his friend?"

She nodded.

"What're they doing about you?"

"They don't see me—just you."

He lay there for what seemed like a really long time, hearing the men's voices, and the thump the plastic-wrapped bricks made when they landed in the back of the buggy.

"They can't see you? Because you live in a tree?"

"Because I'm calling on my tree, yes."

"Your tree," pursued Jason, and *never mind* that girls didn't live in trees, "that has roots in . . . the Land?"

She stared at him, green eyes wide.

"*Yes*," she said.

"Give me your hand."

He raised his, she grabbed it in strong brown fingers.

Immediately his head was flooded with concerned voices, a sense of urgency, a need, a need—

"Hey, what the *hell*!" shouted a man's voice. "Where'd that girl come from?"

Cedar rose, and he did, brought to his feet by her implacable grip. Mr. Varney had just stepped out of the shed, bricks in hand. The other man reached into the buggy's well, and pulled out a gun.

"I accept!" Jason yelled, hanging on to Cedar's hand like it was a lifeline, feeling his roots thrust deep into the soil, and the late sun kissing his leaves. "I accept!"

And he . . .

He threw open his heart.

Joy filled him, the voices swelling into music inside his head. He was stone, he was tree; he was dune rose, cattail, and swamp grass. He was Jason Thibodeau.

He was *Surfside*.

The man by the buggy raised his gun.

Jason . . . *reached*, down below the sand into rock that was Surfside, and snapped it good and sharp, like shaking out a rag rug.

The beach heaved.

Mr. Varney was thrown right off his feet, bricks flying out of his hands. There was a thud, like maybe he'd hit his head on the shed door.

The man with the gun was thrown backward and up, the gun discharging into the air. The buggy flipped over onto its side; the man smacked into it, hard, slid down to the sand, the gun tumbling out of his slack grip, and lay still.

Jason took a deep breath, and looked into Cedar's face.

"OK?" he asked.

She nodded, green eyes glowing.

"Good. Go down to Johnna's and call the sheriff. I'll stay here in case—in case I'm needed."

"Yes," she said, and was gone, running for the boardwalk. Jason sat down in the sand to wait, the voices singing jubilations inside his head.

· · · ·

"WELL, I WON'T SAY THAT was the noisiest thing I ever heard in my life, but it was close."

Jason looked up sharply, seeing the three still forms on the beach, the open door of the shed moving in the sea breeze, the buggy on its side in the sand, the pick-up empty and undisturbed, some distance beyond.

And, suddenly, like a picture slowly coming into focus, a black-haired woman in jeans and a bright blue sweatshirt with the sleeves pushed to the elbow was walking toward him, along the skirt of the dune.

Jason came to his feet.

The woman stopped where she was, maybe a dozen steps out, tucked her hands into the pockets of her jeans while she looked at him, head tipped to one side. *Ride the Carousel at Archers Beach*, was emblazoned across the front of her sweatshirt.

"Pretty damn' impressive," she said. "But still—noisy. What's your name?"

"Jason Thibodeau."

She nodded like she'd sort of expected that, and said, "Well, Jason Thibodeau, I'm Kate Archer, the Guardian next door."

Not too many hours ago, he would've pegged her as a crazy lady with that. Now, he only returned her nod.

"'evening," he said politely. "Sorry about the noise. I'm—new at this."

"No worries, there's only a couple who heard it. Anyhow, I'm not here to complain, but to offer an assist, if you happen to need one." She turned at the waist, looking down at the carnage on the beach.

"You got this under control?"

"I think so. A ... friend went to call the sheriff."

"Good plan. What's the story?"

Jason took a breath.

"The—the dead man, he came looking for Mr. Varney toward the mid-point of my work shift and the two of 'em went to get something out of the shed. When they didn't come back after a time, I got worried and came out to check was everything OK."

She nodded thoughtfully. "And found the scene as it lies before us. Not too bad." She stared down the beach, eyes narrowed. "'less I miss my guess, the dead guy's Remmy Jule, one of our coastline entrepreneurs. The Jules go 'way back, smuggling. Supposing those bricks are marijuana, I don't think the sheriff 's going to have any trouble figuring out what went down here."

She turned back to him, her eyes narrowing as if she'd heard something.

Another heartbeat and Jason heard it, too. A siren.

"You want me to stay?"

He thought about that. "Be hard to explain?"

"It would, at that," she agreed. "You'll do fine. When you get this behind you, look me up, down at the carousel. We can share Guardian tips."

He looked at her, the siren coming closer. Her eyes were green, but human green, and he blurted, "My friend—she . . . lives in a tree."

Kate Archer nodded easily. "So's my grandmother. She tells me it's nice."

She gave him a grin. "I'll leave you to business now, Guardian. Don't be a stranger, hey?"

She walked away then, keeping to the dune's edge until a wisp of sea mist swirled up and hid her from sight.

The siren shrieked into the Sunspray's parking lot, accompanied by squealing tires. He heard a car door slam, and very quickly, the sound of rapid footsteps on the boardwalk.

Jason, Surfside singing in his blood, turned to greet the sheriff.

How Nathan Archer Came to be a Prince of the Land of the Flowers

As told by Kate Archer to Sharon Lee

Y ou might be wondering how it was that Nathan Archer came to be one of the Sasanoa.

The short answer is, he was born in the Land of the Flowers, and raised up in the house of Aeronymous, a Sea Ozali of some considerable standing.

That's the short answer. The longer answer—well, that's a tale.

Now, what you have to understand first off is that the Archers have been on this Land a long, long time. Not as long as the Pepperidges, but—long enough. Some would say, too long. There's various stories in the family about how the Archers came to be caretakers of the Land. Chief Glooskap lost it in a game of dice to the first of the name to settle here—that's one. Another says, no, it was given in return for a favor—and a third still says the other two are hogwash, and what John Archer had done was to marry Glooskap's daughter, with the Land being her wedding portion.

Any of those might be probable, though the giving and losing of land would've been an idea more comfortable with Irish-born John than Glooskap. What Gran says—and I think she has the right of it, myself . . . What Gran says is that John Archer loved this Land so much that the Land loved him back, and gave itself willingly into his keeping, and the keeping of all Archers thereafter.

Gran's also got it in her head that John took a Pepperidge to wife, thereby insuring the immediate continuation of Archers, and beginning the long alliance of the families. I'm not about to argue the point with her.

However it came about, the end result is that the Archers are tied to the Land, bound and intent on insuring its well-being, placing their own safety a distant second to that goal.

That's how it was in the beginning, anyway. Over time, the blood thins and honor with it—humans are like that—and around about 1868, it was looking like the Archers had hit ebb tide.

It wasn't entirely their fault. The Civil War had an appetite for Archer men—not one came back. The wives—widows—they remarried and moved away, taking their little boys, their daughters, and as much of the family silver as they could carry with them. They weren't of the blood anyway, most of 'em. The ones who were left, who were of the blood, they numbered five: Miss Elizabeth and Miss Caroline Archer, maiden ladies of some considerable age; Grampa Richard Archer, who was even older; Daniel Liberty Archer, a babe in arms—and Lydia.

Lydia was twenty-four years old, a spinster with no prospects. She wasn't bad-looking by the standards of the day, more your strapping, sensible Maine girl who in better times would've made some lucky fella a fine wife. The war, though, it had thinned out the available men in town—Archers Beach was a town by then. For every man that came back, there were three women to choose from, and even being an Archer of the Archers, living in the starting-to-run-down house that was held in trust for her baby brother, Lydia never stood a chance.

She cared about that, I'm pretty sure, else what she did that September doesn't really make sense. There's only so much personal sacrifice that a good steward of the Land can be expected to make, and while placing your life between danger and the Land. On the other hand, she may not have understood what she was getting herself—

But, there. I'm getting ahead of the story.

What happened that September in 1868, is that a monster of a storm came boiling up out of Saco Bay, and stood off of Archers Beach like a siege engine, throwing everything it had at the shore. Days, it sat there, never moving, never weakening. Under that onslaught, the town began to come apart. Roofs blew off, carriage houses collapsed; half the boats in the harbor were torn loose from their moorings, and the other half were smashed to flinders.

On the fourth day, at noon, though you couldn't have told it from the light, Lydia Archer left the big house by the kitchen door, and walked down to the sea.

Her bonnet was gone before she'd taken two steps; she was soaked to the bone before she'd gone three. The wind grabbed her hair and like to've pulled it out by the roots, and there was so much water in the air it was a wonder she didn't drown.

Wading knee-deep, leaning her weight into the wind, the rain striking her face hard enough to bruise, Lydia kept walking, and eventually—improbably—she made it to the water's edge. That would have been on the far side of what's now Grand Avenue, with the storm surge chewing at her boots. She hung on to what was left of a hitching post, and she lifted up her face to stare into the storm.

"Stop!" she yelled.

The wind ripped a row of shingles off the wreck of the bandstand and threw them at her. Lydia raised her free hand to shield her face, and when the shingles had fled up the hill, harried by the wind, she yelled at the storm again.

"I'm Lydia Archer and I *command* you to stop!"

Well, that was so novel that the Sea Ozali who was at the core of the disturbance stepped right out of the storm, stood on the turbulent waters and stared down at her, amazed.

"*You*," he said, his sea green curls lying smooth and dry against his brocaded shoulders, "dare to command *me*?"

"In this," Lydia panted, while the storm continued to buffet and abuse her, "I do. I have—precedence."

"Precedence?" Thin green brows lifted in astonishment. "Explain."

"I am—Guardian of the Land," Lydia gasped, as the waves, driven by the wind, leapt up to snatch at her waist.

"Oh, and indeed?" The Sea Ozali was, perhaps, amused. After all, it wasn't every day that he was commanded by *anybody*, much less a mere mortal, who clearly expected it to stick. For a handle on how it must've seemed to him, think about your reaction, if the worms in your springtime garden suddenly rose up on their tails and gave you a piece of their minds.

"How far," he asked, then, because it really was only a game to him, and, truthfully, holding the storm together was beginning to get, just a little, tiresome. "How far, Guardian, will you take your stewardship?"

"As far as necessary," Lydia said, fatefully. "Name your price."

Aeronymous, for it was he, laughed, and the storm began to fray. Hastily, he pulled the trailing edges back, and considered the drenched, ugly mortal, with her brilliant *voysin* – that would be her soul.

"Come with me as my concubine of your own free will, and forsake your Land forever," he said, taunting her. "That is my price."

"And if that is met," gasped Lydia, who was undoubtedly in an altered state by this time, "you will go and leave this Land in peace?"

Aeronymous smiled. "On my name, and on my power, I so swear."

"I'll come," Lydia said, then, "but I have a condition."

"Do you?" he murmured, so entirely diverted that the rain began to lighten from a deluge to a downpour. "And what might that condition be?"

"That any child of our union be given the freedom to return here at their majority, and, if they are wanted, take up the task of Guardian."

"Done!" Aeronymous cried, and held out a hand. "Come to me."

And Lydia—she put her hand in the hand of the Sea Ozali, and walked across the turbulent waves to stand at his side.

He, true to his word, which Ozali can be, now and then—he calmed the waves, dismissed the wind, and stopped the rain. When all was calm and peaceful, and the sun began to glow behind the few remaining rags of clouds, Lydia looked to him, inclined her head—

And Aeronymous snatched them away from Archers Beach, to his palace in the Land of the Flowers, where Lydia did indeed bear him a child before her *voysin* failed and she was gone.

When the boy Nathan reached his majority, Aeronymous, true to his word, as Ozali can be, now and then, set him down in Archers Beach, to determine if the Land required his Guardianship.

It didn't; by 1918 Archers were thick on the ground, and the Land was well taken care of.

However, it was here that Nathan met Nessa Pepperidge, and the two fell in love.

But that's another story.

The Gift of Music

E arly September; the air crisping up, and the sea getting feisty. Fall was bearing down on Archers Beach, and all the rest of Maine, too, the way Andy heard it, but you'd never tell it from the number of folks on the streets, and filling up all the hotels. Folk that'd come up from Away down Boston, and Montreal, Vermont, and New Hampshire. Places Andy'd only heard about, him being Archers Beach, all the way through.

He stood on the Pier, arms folded on the rail, guitar in its case nestled like a dog at his feet. Standing right there, he could look down and see the breakers strike the white beach and splinter into ivory foam. Turning his head just a little, he could see straight up Archer Avenue, all busy with automobiles, and horse-drawn wagons, pedestrians, and the electric trolley just making the turn down from Portland Street.

Well, Andy thought, squinting up the hill against the September sun; it'd be winter soon enough, and the town hunkered down against the cold. Half the hotels would be closed by All Hallow's, and the rest by Thanksgiving Day. Then, it'd be the townies keeping their own company 'til April brought the owners back from their winter places in Portland or Boston. May and April, those were working months, repairing what the winter'd broke, cleaning up, and repainting 'til the town was fit for company again.

He straightened away from the rail, and stretched before reaching down to take the guitar in hand. Truth told, a crowd in town suited him fine; it was always better to play for something other than himself. It was nice to get paid, too, though—another truth told, even at the height of summer there wasn't a lot of work for Andy LaPierre.

The ballroom and the concert halls paid best, but they wanted the Big Bands, and the big acts up from New York and Atlantic City.

A fella like Andy—single fella with a guitar—not much call for him. Less even than a call for a duo—guitar and fiddle, like him and Cray tried doing.

Damn' fool thing, that'd been. That fiddle was dangerous, which they'd both known. Their mistake was in thinking they could handle it—which made them a pair of damnfools.

Fiddle'd almost killed a boy, dancing, at Fathom Five—well, no. Him and Cray'd—*they'd* almost killed the boy, it being them that'd brought the fiddle into it, knowing what it was. And—full truth told—if the boy *had* died, it would've been Andy's death. He was older and he should've been watching; he'd told Cray that he'd *be* watching.

But the fiddle—well. Say the fiddle had its own ideas.

In the end, Andy had come to himself in time, and no lasting harm was done. The boy'd wanted a bracer, and a friendly arm to lean on back to his hotel. Couple of Cray's fingers got burnt, but that wasn't worth mentioning—though Cray still did, now and then, being Cray.

Could've been worse.

It *did* put an end to the duo, though—no real loss. Cray didn't need the music, not like Andy did, and he was happy enough to go back to the marshland and tend his own potatoes.

So that left Andy—a fella and his guitar—playing fill-in, side, and early at the little places, and the speakeasies. Fathom Five, The Pearl and Coral, The Sea Nymph, The Conch—those were his usual venues. Once or twice a summer, he'd pick up a gig at one of the big hotel restaurants, wandering from table to table, playing soft, maybe crooning a little. That was fine, and the tips were good, but the big hotels didn't want the likes of Andy, not regular.

That was all right. It was the music that was important. More important than money. More important than love.

Learning that . . . that'd been a shocker. But the music—it wanted—*it needed*—to be played. It wouldn't let itself be put away to fester. The music—that was his gift, and it wasn't going to let him waste a single note of it.

So, Andy played where they'd have him, for the hat, and supper, sharing his gift, and, just by the way, healing himself.

Tonight, for instance, he was playing The Conch, seven to ten, which was longer than usual, but the sax player's wife had sent a note that he was under the weather. Meaning that he'd drunk too much coffin varnish again.

The word came to Andy's ear about the time it reached Mr. Flannagan, The Conch's barkeep and manager. That meant he was walking in the door, having given the doorman the word, guitar in hand, smoked glasses covering his eyes, before Flannagan had time to send 'round to any of the other regulars. The barkeep didn't necessarily like Andy, which was mutual, but he wasn't a man who relished putting in extra effort, either. Mr. Flannagan didn't like music, and he didn't like musicians, and one was as good as another to him.

Spying Andy, he gave a short nod and turned to draw a beer. "You're playing straight through tonight," he said.

"Yes, sir," said Andy, nice and polite. He took the beer, and went down to the little stage to set up.

He could feel the music buzzing at the ends of his fingers and in-between his ears. He'd just played two days ago, but the music was eager, like there was something special brewing.

He thought about that, tuning up. Something *special*, was it? Well, if that was the case, then it had to be the night was somehow special, 'cause it sure wasn't the gig.

The Conch wasn't one of your upscale places, like the Sea Change or the Casino. But it wasn't just a townie joint, either. Flannagan didn't like townies any more than he liked music or musicians. About the only thing he *did* like was that money from Away. That being so, The Conch made itself agreeable to those folks from Away who had money, but who didn't necessarily expect the digs to be top-notch.

That meant it drew a younger crowd. A tougher crowd. Sometimes, things happened at the Conch that shouldn't've. Flannagan paid a nice percentage of that Away money to the cops, to make sure those things never came to their official notice.

Andy didn't mind the crowd; trouble never came to him that way—and hardly ever came to The Conch when he was playing. The only thing that mattered was that he got to play. Mostly, too, he played for himself; the crowd had their own business, and the sounds he made were background, or less, to them.

That was all right, too; the music did its work. It didn't have to be heard; it only had to be played.

• • • •

HE NOTICED THEM ABOUT half-way through his second set: a couple like any other from Away who owned the kind of money that would make Flannagan's nose twitch. She was pretty, he thought; kinda skinny in a short dress and long beads, a bell-shaped hat cocked over one ear and a big red flower pinned to it. He didn't necessarily incline toward skinny girls, but this one had great, sparkling eyes, and a wonder-smile on her painted mouth. She was hearing the music, no doubt there; hearing it and wanting to hear more.

She made for the empty table to the right of the stage. Her fella followed, but it was plain he wasn't best pleased; jerking his head toward the back o'the room, where there was an arm in the air. Bigger'n her, naturally; burly and thick muscled in a tailored suit; his hair was glossy with brilliantine, slicked back from a square, hard face. He had a little black mustache over a full red mouth, and his hands were square and soft.

He jerked his head again toward the back of the room. The girl pouted. Her fella pulled her chair out with ill-grace, and went to the back of the room alone.

Andy forgot about her for a while then, lost in the music himself. The next time he noticed her was during his supper break. Her fella had come back to her table and was apparently wanting to move on. The girl shook her head, and he grabbed her wrist, jerking her to her feet.

Andy came away from the bar fast, meaning to have a word with the boy, but—she looked right at him; met his eyes like she could see them behind the dark lenses . . .

. . . and shook her head.

He nodded, slightly, and went back to his supper, watching as her fella pulled her arm through his, and they moved toward the door. It seemed she went willing, and her fella stayed civilized, 'til they were out of his sight, gone into the breezy September night.

Andy sighed, still feeling unsettled, which was just foolishness. He didn't have nothing to do with people from Away. Nothing to do at all.

• • • •

HE AMUSED HIMSELF WITH a run of old ballads: "Low Bridge," "Old Dan Tucker," "Big Rock Candy Mountain"—nobody noticed. Nobody ever did. He played 'til it was time to stop playing, got the guitar into its case, and drank a last beer while Flannagan counted out the hat.

Two dollars and eighty-five cents; more than he'd expected from this crowd. He left fifty cents on the bar, so Mr. Flannagan wouldn't find him to be lacking in gratitude, stowed the rest in his pockets and strolled down the noisy, crowded room. The guy on the door opened up for him; he nodded his thanks, and followed the smoke out into the sweet autumn air.

• • • •

HE WALKED DOWN THE hill, among the glare of the electric lights. Despite the hour, the streets were crowded; the light spilling from the new hotels making the street as bright as day. Down at the bottom of the hill was the Pier, hung with so many lights it looked like a sun had fallen into the sea. Andy could hear the band playing at the Casino—Paul Whiteman's Orchestra, it was this weekend—nice and clear.

He ambled along, in no rush to be anywhere, guitar case over his shoulder, weighing whether he wanted to go over to the Casino and take in what was left of the show. Might learn something.

Or might not. He didn't much care for the Big Band sound, and while some of the arrangements might be adapted for a single fella and his guitar, most were built for that full orchestra.

Be a lot more to learn at the jam session, after the Pier closed down for the night and honest folk were asleep. That was when the roadies, and some of the orchestra musicians, too—the ones who lived the music almost like Andy did—they'd get together to play. Blues, now, there was something a fella and his guitar could learn from the Blues. Might be good to sit in, tonight. Nothing else doing, after all.

It was right about then that he noticed her, keeping pace with him on the crowded walk, a careful arm's length away.

Andy stopped. The girl stopped, too, and turned to face him. Her big eyes were bright under the brim of the perky little hat—bright and hard as glass. He could see her shivering, which was no surprise. September it might be, and mild, yet, but they were still on the Maine coast, and the wind off the ocean wanted a shawl or a jacket to turn it.

"Best you go inside," he told her, gentle, because it took some that way, those who really *heard* the music, and they got confused about what it was they wanted. "I've got nothing for you, missy."

"But you do." Her voice was husky, and it shivered, too. "Have something for me."

Well. Maybe he'd misjudged. He looked at her dress, the pearls, and the earrings. Expensive things, by his reckoning.

"You want money?" he asked.

"Money?" she repeated blankly, then swept her hand out, as if tossing the word, or a coin, away. "I don't care about money."

"Right, then. You go on back to your room, wherever you're staying."

Her hard, brilliant eyes widened, and she lunged, catching his sleeve.

"No!" she said sharply, and then, more moderately, "No, I can't go back there. Please—please walk with me, just down to the trolley stop."

They were blocking the sidewalk, or should've been. People flowed past without seeing them, no smallest shift of the eyes to acknowledge their presence. That was right, most folk didn't see him, unless he wanted them to, which he didn't, right at present, and they'd automatically look away from a girl who was talking to herself.

Still, seemed the best thing to do was ease off the don't-see-me, and get her out of the way before some drunk trampled her, or a fella with an eye to opportunity decided she was too crazy to know what was happening to her.

"Sure," he said. "I'll walk you down. Best step it up; last trolley for Portland leaves at midnight."

"I know," she said, and, "thanks."

He waited for her to let go his sleeve, but she didn't, just stood there looking at him, shivering in the breeze—or maybe, he thought suddenly, not only with the breeze.

"Where's your fella?" he asked her.

She blinked. "Gone drinking with Percy. I told him I was tired, and wanted to go back to the hotel to sleep."

He nodded, and, when she still didn't move, or let go of him, he turned and started walking again, down the hill.

She went with him, drawing closer, and slipping her hand into the crook of his arm, like they were walking out together. That hurt, that did, and he almost pulled himself free of her.

"You can, can't you?" she said breathless and shaky before he could pull away. "You can . . . fix things."

He felt a thrill; a stronger repeat of the sensation he'd had earlier, that there was *something special* about to happen. He'd seen that the girl heard the music; that she'd also been able to puzzle out the music's purpose—well. There were those who could see the wyrd and understand the strange, even though they, themselves, were neither.

Her question wanted answering, though, and he had to be careful with it.

"I can't fix anything," he said, and felt the sour truth in his belly.

"Not you, maybe," she said, talking fast, now; her words tumbling over each other like puppies. "The guitar—the *music*—that's it, isn't it? I felt it, back there in the bar. I felt it begin to—to stitch me together." Her laugh was even less steady than her voice.

"Stitch me together, that was it. Like a kid's rag doll."

"Look, missy," he said. "Whatever you want—"

"I want you—the music—I want . . . to be fixed. It—the music—it can do that, can't it?"

She'd found the twist, bless the girl. *He* couldn't fix one blessed thing, true enough, but the music—that was something else.

Careful again, he said, "It can't *fix*. Not the way you're thinking, it can't." He hesitated, and threw her a glance.

That was a mistake. Her face was rosy, her eyes on fire; the bright red mouth pinched until it was hardly pink.

"What's the trouble?" he asked, the words drawn unwilling out of him, one by one.

"I just want to get away, that's all!" she said, her fingers digging into his arm like a vise. "But he has the stuff, and he—I—if I don't have it, I'll die."

He knew then, why her eyes were so bright, and why she shivered so.

"Your fella gives you dope?" he asked.

She nodded, jerkily.

"It was—swell at first, y'know? But it didn't stay swell. I'm sick of it—and I'm sick without it."

"That's how it goes with the dope," Andy said, and it was pity he felt for her, knowing now why she was so thin. "Nothing to fix it, that I ever heard."

"If I can get away," the girl said. "Go up to Portland. I got—I got an old school chum in Portland. She'll help me."

"Then you don't need me," he said. "Last trolley to Portland's at midnight."

"I know that, don't I? Or why'd I ask you to walk me to the stop?"

"You said you wanted to be fixed," he reminded her.

"Fixed—I need; I need to stay strong enough—to not go back—to get on that trolley and get to Sarah."

It wouldn't do her any good, and might hurt Sarah, too, depending on how deep the dope had a grip. Not his problem; he told himself. He had nothing to do with folks from Away.

He sighed, lightly, and put his hand over her fingers that were leaving bruises on his arm.

"I'll wait with you," he told her. "And I'll maybe play some while we wait."

Hope flared in those too-bright eyes. "Thank—"

"No, now, hear me out! There's no fixing involved. Music might put a little courage in you, maybe. *Maybe*. And not so much as that."

When she crossed out of Archers Beach—well, he didn't know what happened to the music's power, outside of Archers Beach, now did he?

"Courage enough to hold you on the trolley," he said, not promising it—not exactly. "So you'll sit tight, all the way into the city. Get a taxi to your friend. Understand me . . . " He paused, thinking how best to tell her that distance wasn't what she needed; that she was carrying her doom inside her—she was sick, he recalled her saying. Well, then, she knew as much as he did.

"Sylvia," she said, shaking him out of his thoughts.

He looked down into her face again.

"What?"

"Sylvia. It's my name."

He felt it strike him, solid, like a fist against the heart, and almost swore. Dammit, he hadn't asked for her name!

Asked or not; he had it, now. And everything that went with it.

He sighed.

"Dangerous thing to be giving your name out to anybody," he said, mild, like it made no difference.

"You're not anybody," she answered. A breath, and she added, "You don't have to tell me yours."

Damn right, he didn't have to tell her his.

"Cross here," is what he said, and took them across Archer Avenue, to Milliken.

"Trolley stops on Grand," Sylvia objected.

"Stops on Milliken first, and it's quieter there. You want the music to concentrate on you, right?"

She nodded, jerkily. "Right."

The town council had planted fewer street lights on Milliken, it being a secondary way. There was plenty of spill off of Archers Avenue, though, and a lamp post right next to the trolley stop, its light furry in the sea-damp air.

Andy settled into the corner of the little wooden bench, and slipped the guitar out of its case. He could feel the music buzzing in his fingers; buzzing in his head. It came on like that, sometimes, 'specially if he hadn't played in a while. After a night of moving music through him . . . it worried him a little, just while he was getting the case out of the way and settling his fingers along the strings. It worried him, that the music was so eager, almost like it . . . had a plan.

It *ought* to worry him, that the music had a plan, but once he had his fingers on the frets, nothing worried him at all.

"Sit on down," he murmured. "We got a couple minutes."

"I don't want to sit down!" she snapped, and he might've snapped back, but there wasn't any sense to it—it was the dope making her twitchy and mad.

"Suit yourself."

His fingers were already moving, teasing out a melody—"Simple Gifts," it was. Good music, that one; gentle. Powerful.

What it felt like, playing the music—the kind and style of music he played . . . It felt like . . . it felt like he went all still at the dead center of him while light filled him up, flowing out through his fingers to wash away the pain and sadness around him.

That was why he'd stopped playing, after Nessa married her prince and took herself off to the Land of the Flowers. He'd told her that he was happy, so long as she was happy—but that'd been a lie.

The truth was, it felt like his heart'd been torn out, and there was no still place inside him for the light to fill up. He'd gone back to his land, threw himself into its care and keeping, not thinking; only serving.

Until the night he found himself standing on the corner of Milliken and Archer, hat on the ground by his feet, his fingers bleeding from the strings—playing.

Playing.

That had hurt—the music melting the scar tissue; growing him a new heart. It had hurt for a long time, but he learned. He learned to let the music—what the music was and everything that it did—fill him up and flow away. It was his gift—his gift to give away.

It was rare that he played just for one person. The full power of the music focused on a single heart and soul—not many could bear that. When he'd been young, and learning his gift, he'd broken a man's heart, playing just to him. His fault; he hadn't known the limits of a human heart, then. Still didn't, though he had a far shrewder notion.

He learned to play for big groups; he'd learned to give the music away to the street, to a meadow, to the sea—and to those strong enough to bear it.

This girl now, this Sylvia—she was only human, wyrd-sighted though she seemed. Whole and healthy, she wasn't strong enough to bear the full brunt of the music; sick with the dope like she was, and dying—the best thing the music could do, to *fix* her, like she wanted, was to kill her outright, and stop her from hurting any more.

His fingers moved along the frets without him paying any particular mind, and it was "Shenandoah" this time, easing into the space that had been warmed by "Simple Gifts." Andy looked up, wanting to see how she was bearing it—but what he saw was the music, swirling 'round and through her, lighting her up like she was a candle.

A funny kind of candle, with the flame guttering, and a space of blackness before there was light again, burning brilliant and brave.

He watched, his fingers moving up and down the strings; he watched the music coil around the brilliant base of the candle and . . . tighten. The light moved up, slow, like the dark patch was almost too heavy to budge.

The music tightened again. He found his fingers insistent, and it was some Spanish thing now, that he'd learned from that sailor, long winters ago. Flamenco, thrumming hard and insistent, exerting pressure, until the white base of the candle flowed upward into the darkness, and the crowning flame flared bright blue-white.

The bottom half of the candle—that was dark, now, and Andy's fingers slowed, sliding out of insistence into a gentle murmur; not music, really; more like whistling to yourself when you'd just done something that scared you bad.

The music flowed away, the image of the candle faded, and it was just the girl, Sylvia, standing there and staring at him, her face a little pale now, and her eyes soft with tears.

"You fixed me," she whispered. "I felt—"

"You felt," he said, his voice a harsh counterpoint to the murmur of the music. "You felt half your life taken off the back end, and applied to the front. You won't die this week, missy, but you won't live out the length you was given."

Her mouth tightened, the lipstick long gone, and then she nodded, once, firmly enough that the brave red flower on her hat jerked with it.

"But I was *going* to die this week, wasn't I?"

"Can't say that, missy, but you were in a bad way."

"Then I'll take that shorter span," she said firmly, and stiffened her thin shoulders.

"What're you gonna do, then?"

"Like I said. Go to Portland; find Sarah. Figure out what to do with what I've got left."

A bell sounded, around a crackle of electricity. Sylvia looked over her shoulder.

"The trolley's here," she said, but instead of moving toward the curb, she stepped up to the bench, leaned down and kissed his cheek.

"Thank you," she said. "I mean that."

She turned, then, took a step, turned back to look at him, a wry grin on her pale face.

"I don't have car fare."

He snorted lightly, and came to his feet, one hand still fondling the strings while he dug into his pocket and pulled out his evening's earnings.

"Here."

"That's too much!"

"Taxi ride to Sarah, once you're in Portland," he said. "Something to eat, maybe."

He pushed the money at her. "I'll get more, tomorrow."

She laughed. "You talked me into it."

The trolley arrived with a clang of the bell; the door clattered open.

"Milliken Street!" the conductor yelled. "All aboard for Portland, Congress Street Car Barn!"

A fella came down the stairs, none-too-steady on his feet, tipped his hat in Sylvia's general direction—"Miss."—and charted an uncertain route down Milliken, taking the corner wide at Imperial, and heading up the hill, toward the boarding houses.

Sylvia mounted one step, and stopped to look over her shoulder at him.

"Come with me," she said.

He shook his head, both hands on the strings, and the music moving softly out into the night.

"Got everything I need, right here."

"Lucky you," she said.

"Hey!"

Andy turned, fearing the worst—and here it came, the fella she'd been with at The Conch, hatless and running.

"Sylvia! Hey! Hold that trolley!"

She froze; she half-turned . . . "Jake?"

Andy brought his hand across the strings in a slash, waking discord. "Go!" he shouted, and used what she'd freely given him against her.

"Sylvia! Get on the trolley!"

Her body stiffened. Wooden, but obedient to his command, she mounted the steps. The doors clashed shut behind her. Electricity crackled; sparks danced along the wire.

"Hey!"

The fella—Jake—slammed to a stop by the bench, breathing hard, and shaking his fist at the trolley's backside.

"Evenin', Jake," Andy said, quiet and firm. The man turned toward him, eyes widening.

"You—What'd you do with my girl?"

"Gave her some help. She asked me."

"Yeah? Well, you're gonna be sorry you did that. How about I break that guitar over your head?"

"No," Andy said, and heard the music coming out of the guitar, thick and dark and heavy.

He tried to stop, but the music had him as much as it had Jake, and the music was *angry*.

"You better leave," he told Jake, and tried to change it; to play something else. He thought the notes of "Simple Gifts;" but his fingers continued to call forth darkness and doom. The strings were icy against his skin, and he saw the music flow into the man and through him.

Saw the candle—saw, Andy thought, the man's *soul*—dull and tarnished thing that it was, with its flame guttering orange.

His fingers were pitiless; they played on, and the dark music swept out in an eddy so poisonously perfect that Andy felt the tears prick his eyes.

There was no filling here; no squeezing, neither. Just a breeze, that was all, cold, and soft, and sudden.

The candle flame flickered, guttered . . . and licked back up, just a glow now . . .

Andy drew a breath; he drew deep, on all the power he had in him.

He lifted his hand away from the strings.

The music stopped.

The man's guttering soul flickered in the passing of the cold breeze; Jake swayed—then straightened as the flame steadied and flared.

"You . . . " he snarled again, taking a step forward.

Andy slashed his hand across the strings, making them scream.

"Run!" he shouted. "Jake, you better run away—and forget you knew Sylvia!"

He felt that last bit take, just before Jake jumped like he'd been poked with a hot wire. A harsh gasp, near enough to a scream, got loose from him, and his slick-soled shoes scraped the sidewalk as he sprang into a run, up Milliken, back toward the lights of Archers Avenue.

Andy watched until Jake was just one more silhouette among the many up on the Avenue. Then, he walked over to the bench and put his guitar away in its case.

He stood for a little while, then, shivering; the breeze off the ocean having gone from chilly to cold.

"Shows what comes of dealing with folks from Away," he said, to nobody in particular.

He sighed, and slung the case over his shoulder, looking toward home.

Midnight, he thought. The Big Band would be finishing up its last set real soon, and the jam session'd be warming up. He wanted voices around him, and music, that was what.

Tonight, now, he thought, moving slow toward Archer Avenue.

Tonight, he'd learn to play the Blues.

The night don't seem so lonely

"And that was Yellow Submarine by the fab four, also known as—THE BEATLES!" The DJ's voice evaporated into a cloud of static, and came back, a little watery now:

". . . listening to WKOX-FM, one-oh-five-point-seven, Framingham, Mass. All rock, all

the—"

More static, fizzing loud.

"Jesus Christ!" Ben swore. "Find another station, willya, Mossie?"

Moss leaned forward, fiddling with the dial, picking up a lot of static, and a thin line of what might've been "Crystal Blue Persuasion," though it was hard to tell in the rush of road noise coming in the open windows.

He upped the volume just in time for the thread of song to dissolve into a loud honk of noise.

"Christ!" Ben swore again, his hand flashing out.

Moss ducked—not that Ben had hit him, yet—and the music clicked off.

"Goddamn dead zone," Ben said. "You wait'll we get to Portland. Got a stereo set up, all the records you can listen to: Beatles, Stones, Dylan, Doors—all the good stuff. You'll like it just fine."

Moss had heard this before—Ben had picked him up a couple miles south of the Mass Pike, so they'd been together almost a day. The story was that Ben shared a house in Portland, Maine, on India Street. The plan—Ben's plan—was for Moss to come home with him, and "help out" for crash space and food.

It was a nice plan, Moss thought—for Ben. He didn't particularly have anything against Ben, mind. The man'd been more than fair with him: fed him a couple burgers, with fries, made sure he had a new, cold Coke every time they stopped for gas, offered to share his cigarettes and his reefers, too; and had only wanted one blow-job, which he'd asked for, nice and polite. His momma would've liked Ben.

Well, and Momma never did have no sense in men; which was the reason Moss was sixteen, and hitchin', and givin' blow-jobs to such folk as might pick him up. Momma'd taught him it was wrong to be beholden, so he made sure him and his rides were caught up even by the time he left 'em.

. . . though that was lookin' like it might be a problem, with Ben, here. Moss had no intention of letting himself be took into a strange house in a strange city and set to work givin' blow-jobs—or worse—to them he owed nothing to—or maybe Ben had the idea he'd like to deliver reefers, which he wouldn't much care for, neither.

Trouble was, they were getting close to Portland—he'd seen a sign 'bout ten miles back that said 38 miles, which meant he was going to have to give Ben the slip at the next gas stop.

He glanced over at the dash. Gauge was showing under a quarter, and the way this old Lincoln drank down the gas, no way they were making even twenty-five more miles without a top-off.

"Be home for dinner," Ben said, maybe thinking he was looking at the odometer. "We'll stop and pick up some groceries—beer, Coke, whatever you like—'fore we get there. Sound good to you, Mossie?"

"Sure," he said, and smiled, because Ben would want him to smile and be excited about comin' inside to a regular house where there was a shower, and regular meals an' all. A place where he could be useful and maybe earn some money and not have to put up with Momma's new boyfriend whaling on him, and calling him a freak and a weakling, and yelling at him to *die, already*.

His momma—give her credit—she hadn't liked seein' her boyfriend smacking her sickly son around, so she'd done what she could, since she wasn't going to be givin' the boyfriend up no time soon, not with a new baby on the way. She'd given Moss his own daddy's backpack, from when he'd been in the Army, and she'd told him to pack up his clothes and any other little thing that was his. Then, she'd given him nineteen dollars, which was all the grocery money, drove him out to the edge of the city, so the cops wouldn't give him no hassle, opened the door and told him to go.

He gave her back a ten, because he knew she'd want to think well of herself, and remember that she hadn't sent him out empty-handed. The boyfriend, though, he'd still expect to eat, and there wasn't no sense her getting the man mad when she'd just done him a good turn.

She took the money quick enough that he knew she'd been counting on him giving some back. He picked up his pack from between his feet, and got out of the car.

"Moshe," she said, just as he was shutting the door.

"Ma'am?"

"You remember now—don't you walk too hard, or too far. You mind your heart. Promise me."

"I promise, Momma," he said, giving her a smile to show he didn't mind it; and closed the door nice and soft.

By the time he'd gotten to the end of the parking lot, she was gone.

"We'll pull over for gas just up the road," Ben said, breaking into Moss's thoughts. "Get us some Cokes and chips to last the rest of the way."

Moss looked out the window, saw a long main street like a lot he'd seen in New England—hardware store, five and dime, diner . . . and 'way up the end of the block, on the right, a white, red and blue Esso sign.

"Where are we?" he asked, 'cause of course the hardware store was somebody's name, which wasn't no help, and the diner was The Golden Rooster, with a big sign in the front window that said, "Something to Crow About!"

"Saco," Ben said. "That bridge we just come across was the Saco River. Town just the other side was Biddeford."

"And next is Portland?"

"Nah. Still gotta do the rest of Saco, then Scarborough, then over the bridge into the city. Twenty miles, maybe. Home for dinner, just like I said."

This was definitely the place for him to get off.

Moss smiled. "Sounds great," he said.

Ben pulled up to the pumps, and cut the engine. Moss opened his door.

"Gotta hit the head," he said. He closed the door briskly and walked to the office.

"Key?" he said to the guy behind the counter.

"Over there on the hook," the guy said, jerking his head to the left without bothering to look around.

Moss snagged the one labeled "M" and was out the door, ducking past Ben as he came in, and scooting around the side of the building.

But he didn't go to the men's room. He tucked the key on its piece of wood in the back pocket of his jeans, and looked around the corner at the car.

There was only one guy on, and he'd put the pump on automatic while he got under the hood to check the oil.

Good, thought Moss. It was time to leave Ben and get on alone. He couldn't risk the house on India Street, not by a long damn, he couldn't. Sure, he was on the street, and he didn't have an address, but he'd talked to the other kids he'd met on his way out from KC. Some of 'em—a lot of 'em—they'd made mistakes, and they were willing to share what they'd done wrong, or seen done wrong, what and who to look out for ...

He didn't quite have Ben figured, but that didn't matter. The only kind of person who picked up a hitcher, treated him good, and promised him a nice room in his own home—was the kind of person no hitcher wanted to know. Might be Ben was on good behavior until they got to that house, which might not even be his. Some places, after they had a kid for a while, they sent him out to get more kids ...

Well.

Wasn't here nor there, really. He had a plan—he had a duty—and he was gonna see it done. He'd promised.

Moss slipped around the back of the car, opened the back door, ducked inside and grabbed the strap of his backpack.

Easing the door closed, he looked to the front, but the gas guy was still fiddling around with the engine. He stood on tiptoes to look over the roof of the Lincoln; saw Ben in the window, talking with the office man, but shifting a little like Ben did when he was nervous. Might be he was starting to wonder how long Moss was gonna take.

Time to go.

He fished the key out of his back pocket and dropped it onto the tarmac, then slung the pack over his shoulder, ducking a little to be sure he was below the line of the car's roof, and angled toward the shrubs and trees lining the edge of the station.

He'd just gotten past the shrubs and was almost into the trees when he heard somebody running behind him, and Ben's voice yelling.

"Hey! Hey! Moss! You come back here, you little—Hey! Somebody help me catch that kid, he's got my wallet!"

That didn't take long.

Moss pushed further into the trees, wondering how deep the little wood was.

Behind, there came some crashing and snapping as branches broke, and Ben yelling, "C'mon Moss, quit foolin' around; we gotta go!" and the gas guy maybe it was yelling, "C'mon, kid; the boss is calling the cops. Just throw the guy's wallet out here and everything's square."

"What the hell you talkin' about?" Ben yelled. "He's with me!"

"Thought he had your wallet."

"Well, he does. He. . .plays these jokes. But we're together. Mossie! C'mon, it ain't funny no more."

No, thought, Moss, it wasn't. Up ahead, flashing silver through the leaves, he saw a chain link fence. Behind him, they were still crashing, and to the right . . .

To the right, it was downhill and more trees and maybe he could lose them, if he ran like hell.

• • • •

HE DROPPED TO HIS KNEES in a little clearing, panting for air and his heart pounding funny like it did, and there were little spikes of pain in his chest, and he just put his palms flat against the dirt, and hoped that this wasn't it, the time that his bad heart went bust on him, and then he hoped that it was, it hurt so bad, and then . . .

. . . he woke up to the soft inquiry of an owl, and stars above him, between the leaves. He was tired, but nothing hurt, and he took a deep breath of the cool, damp air, tasting salt.

The ocean, that must be. He was close to the ocean—the Atlantic Ocean, that was. He'd struck out deliberate for the Atlantic Ocean, all those weeks ago, on account of his duty. His promise to his dad. 'course, his dad'd thought—had said!—that Moss would make good on the promise when he was a man.

Wasn't dad's fault that Moss wasn't likely to live that long. He hadn't caught the fever 'til after dad was gone himself. Strep throat, that was what they thought . . .

Well.

Water under the bridge. His dad used to say that. *That's just water under the bridge, Moshe, all flowed away and gone.*

That was what happened to the bad things—they all flowed away, to the ocean, and the ocean salt dissolved them. Try to carry the bad things around, and they'd weigh you down into the ground.

The good things, though, you carried them with you, 'cause good things, they didn't weigh no more than sunlight.

The owl hooted again, softer, like maybe it was telling him to go back to sleep; he was safe here.

Moss took another deep breath, smiling at the lack of pain. Tomorrow, he thought drowsily, he'd find the ocean.

• • • •

THE SAND ON THE BEACH was just like his dad had told him, white, like snow; fine as flour. Surely was pretty, but it was tricky to walk in. His sneakers were sliding and his knees were working, and it was hard to make any headway. He did it, though he was panting like a grampaw, and his heart was kinda beating strange, one thump harder than the next two. No pain, though, so he didn't mind it, much.

What his dad hadn't told him about, though, was how the air smelled—not just salty, but fresh, like air right after a thunderstorm. Smelling it made him feel like dancing, though maybe not in the dry sand.

Finally, he made it to wet sand. He could walk better now, almost like on a sidewalk, and he kept on going, to where the waves come in, rolling soft and slow, and every one that found the sand making a sweet little *plash*.

Moss stood there, looking out over the bright, glittery, gently rolling waters, and he felt something happen in his chest—not pain, or that squeezing thing that sometimes happened. No. . .it felt, somehow like he was happy—too happy to laugh.

So happy, his stupid heart wanted him to cry. Well . . .

He slung the pack around and lowered it to the sand, then knelt and undid the buckle.

There, in the hidden pocket underneath the right back pocket, he found the little pouch, and pulled it out.

For a long time, they'd just sat out on a shelf in his room, but when Momma's new boyfriend moved in, Moss had thought maybe it would be better to empty his old shooters out into his sock drawer, and put his dad's tokens into the bag, outta sight.

The bag, he tucked under his t-shirts, and the boyfriend never found it to break, though he'd broken some other stuff he had no business putting his hands on . . .

Moss closed his eyes and took a breath.

Water under the bridge, he told himself, all flowed away and gone.

Leaving the pack where it was, he walked down to the place where the little waves kissed the beach. There were shells, here and there on the wet sand; strings of weed, and stones as shiny as living eyes.

Just by his foot were two flat, round bones, beige-brown and laying together in the damp. *Sand dollars*, they were called, his dad had told him, on account they looked like big ol' silver dollars. The two on the beach were damp, and gritty with sand, and though they looked stiff, he knew that they were living critters.

The one he took outta his pouch, though, that one was white as bone, the critter long dead. He put it on the wet sand near the two live ones, and then reached into the bag for the couple other shells, scattering them onto the sand from his fingertips as he walked a little ways down the waterline.

When the bag was empty, he upended it, so any sand and grit and pieces could fall out, then shoved it into his pocket.

He took a deep breath, looking out over the water, and sighed.

Duty done. Promise kept. The lazy, rolling water glittered a little more, like maybe he'd caught some drops on his eyelashes.

Another breath, and here came a roller that was taller than the others, seeming to move a little faster, too. Before he could figure out how that might be, it struck the sand with a *boom*! White spray flew into the air, splashing his face, then the wave was gone, leaving Moss with his jeans wet and his sneakers soggy. The sand around him, where he'd left the shells and the dead sand dollar, was clean, just like somebody had reached out a hand and swept them off the beach.

• • • •

"HERE HE COMES BACK, now," Felsic said, leaning on the ticket counter under Noah's Ark.

Phyllis didn't bother to look up from her newspaper.

"Lost boy from Away got nothing to do with me. Or with you."

"Might be he's not lost," Felsic said; "that's what's nagging at me."

Phyllis rattled the paper.

"Says here, next month, NASA's gonna be trying to land on the moon. Think o'that, now, eh?"

"Quite an age we live in," Felsic said agreeably.

The boy'd been down to the sea; his jeans was wet to the knee, and his sneakers squelched on the land. Might've made an offering—he had the look of it. Gone down heavy, come back light. Wasn't nothing more keeping that boy from floating off to the moon his own self, now that the sea'd taken what he'd brought to it.

"Hungry," Felsic said, because Phyllis wasn't near as cold as she talked, and she was listenin', even if she was pretendin' not to be lookin'.

"Give 'im a job," Felsic urged; "can't hurt."

Phyllis sighed gustily, rattled the paper closed, and stared across the parking lot at the kid an' his backpack an' the dazed way he was starin' around.

"All right," she snapped. "I'll give 'im a job, if he wants one, but I ain't chasing 'cross the parkin' lot to hand it to 'im. He gets his tail over here like a sensible boy, and looks at the board, then—all right."

"Fine," Felsic said soothingly. "That's fine."

A little ripple, that's all it took, the boy might be from Away, but he wasn't one o'the deaf-and-blind ones. No, he felt the ripple, took the suggestion into his head, and started moving 'cross the lot, toward the Ark, and the signboard over at the side saying *Operators Wanted*.

Phyllis saw him moving, took note of his direction and turned a pretend glare on Felsic.

"Well, *boss*?" she asked, sarcastic, but that was just her way. "Where you puttin' him?"

"Jack 'n Jill," said Felsic promptly. "Sally'll do 'im a world o'good."

• • • •

SALLY WAS A LITTLE bit something: she teased, and laughed, climbed up the outside scaffolding like a cat, expecting him to keep up. His momma would've said she was "lively." Moss thought she might be something more—or other—than just that. Her eyes flashed yellow in the shadow sometimes, like cat-eyes. She slipped a little, climbing ahead of him, and he thought he saw claws come out from the tips of her fingers and snag the canvas awning stretched between the slide and Noah's Ark.

Still and all, he liked her—claws and cat-eyes, too. She'd come back down the scaffold to him when he'd had to rest in his climb, an' asked what was the matter.

"Little breathy; need a quick rest. I got a tricky heart," he told her, which was more than he told most people, for fear of being laughed at. "Had rheumatic fever when I was a little kid."

"That mean you shouldn't climb?" she asked. "'cause, if you want, we can just set you down at the gate t'take admission. I can do what climbing needs done."

There now—*that* was why he liked her. She didn't make fun, and she didn't disbelieve, or go tell Boss Phyllis he was *sick*, either; just offered up a plan for how to work the ride out between 'em.

"I can climb; just sometimes I gotta rest."

"OK, then," she said, and perched on the bar above him, easy as a cat, until he started climbing again.

Up at the top of the slide, standing on the platform, you could see everything there was to see in Archers Beach and beyond—the sun glittering on the ocean, and the land curving, miles away. He could see it all, despite the glittery sea and the fresh damp air making his eyes water. Sally got him turned around so he could look up the hill at the stores and the people shopping, and the cars and delivery trucks doing business.

"This is my favorite place," Sally said, close in his ear, like she was telling him a secret. "You can see *every*thing."

Well, you couldn't see Kingman, Kansas, but maybe that was all right, too. Moss took a deep, deliberate breath of wonderful air, and smiled.

"Sure is fine," he said, and Sally laughed.

"Where're you from?"

"Kansas," he said. Sally frowned like he'd said something foreign.

"Much like here?" she asked.

"Not anything like here."

"What brings you to us, then?"

He shook his head, his eyes damp from the sun striking off all that moving blue water.

"Made a promise to my dad. He was here, years back. Picked up some shells and stuff on the beach. He gave 'em to me, before he died, and said that I had to go to Archers Beach when I was grown up, and give the shells back to the sea. Made me promise. So, I come to fill the promise."

Sally didn't make a fuss about that, either, or tell him he was silly. He had the feeling that Sally took promises serious, and he liked her even more.

"Be going back soon?"

Going back? thought Moss. What would he go back for? Or to? He shook his head.

"I think I'll stay here. I think . . . my dad wanted me to see something different. He told me how, when he first saw the Atlantic Ocean, he said it changed his whole life, and how he saw the world."

"He went back, though," Sally said, looking down at the parking lot below them.

"He did, yeah. He'd made his own promise, that he would go back. He was married to my mother."

Sally nodded, still staring down.

Moss looked up, into the deep blue sky. A shadow flashed over his face, and a seagull screamed. Music started from somewhere—sounded like merry-go-round music.

"We gotta get down," Sally said. "Park's opening for the day."

He did look down, then, thinking about the climb before him, and trying to guess would his chest seize again, like it'd done on the way up.

"We'll take the easy way down," Sally said, picking up a rough-wove mat, and dropping it flat to the platform.

"Here," she said. Moss blinked. "Sit down!"

She sounded a little impatient, suddenly, so he dropped to the mat—and gasped when she hit him between the shoulder blades. He yelled, the mat skidded forward, tipped—and hit the slide.

Wind rushed past his ears as the mat picked up speed. He yelled again, and the rushing air snatched his voice away with the rest of his breath, and he was flying, flying toward the ground in a grand, speeding spiral, and he leaned in the next curve, deliberately increasing his speed, chest aching, and the salty breeze in his mouth, and there was the end of the slide, and a stocky figure in a cap at the end of it, and just beyond a pile of sawdust, and he was airborne, sawdust erupting in a fragrant cloud. He collapsed, gasping, until strong arms came around and half-dragged him up and away.

"Can't stay there, boy; we got incomin'," somebody—Felsic—said, propping him up against a sturdy shoulder. He heard a yell over the laboring bellows of his heart and here came Sally, her mat already airborne, and she was out, over the edge, hitting the sawdust and waking an explosion. Pine scent enveloped him and he coughed, grabbing at his chest, and it was glorious, and it hurt . . . it hurt . .

. . . nothing hurt at all.

He was laying on the ground, in the shade next to the end of the slide. His head was on Sally's knee, and Felsic was bent over him, one hand on his chest. He didn't hurt anymore, but only felt kind of light and cool.

"What's the matter with you, deah?" Felsic murmured.

Moss tried to marshal words out of the vast sense of cool peace, but Sally was quicker.

"He said he's gotta tricky heart," she said. "Needed a breather, part way up, climbin'."

"Rheumatic fever," Moss managed, so they had the right name of it. And if it meant that he couldn't work here, couldn't stay here, then he'd rather die—

"Don't fatch," Felsic said, and Moss felt the rising panic reverse, and just drain away.

"That's it," Felsic said. "You rest a spell. Sal—you go open up. Moss'll be along shortly."

"All right," she said, and Moss felt lips, cool and slightly damp, pressed against his cheek, before she moved his head from her lap to something else soft, and he heard her sneakers scuffing on the tarmac.

"I can work," Moss said, though without any urgency. "Don't want the boss mad at me, right off."

"She's fine." Felsic leaned back, hand slipping into a pocket. "This heart business . . ."

"Means I'm gonna die. But not today."

"Well, then. That's all any of us got, ain't it? You sit up all right?"

He did, with Felsic's help, and a couple minutes later, he stood under the same conditions.

"I'm good," he said. "I can work." Felsic nodded and stood.

"Up to Sally, o'course, but don't be surprised you're on ticket-box today."

"If that's where she needs me . . ."

A gong sounded, loud; somewhere nearby a mule brayed in either complaint or approval.

"That's my call to the Coal Mine," Felsic said. "You go on, an' be good, right?"

"Right."

• • • •

THE RIDES CLOSED AT eight o'clock. Moss went to get his pack from where he'd stowed it, in Boss Phyllis' office.

"Sally said you did good today," the boss said. "You comin' back tomorrow?"

"Yes, ma'am. I'll come every day you need me."

She gave him a once-over at that, like she heard what he hadn't said, but all she said was, "Showers in the White Way, next door. You hungry, you stop at Bob's over at Grand and Dube and tell 'em behind the counter that you work for me. Same thing tomorrow breakfast."

Moss looked at her careful.

"That's included in, or comes outta my pay?"

"Included in. That *all right* by you, deah?"

"Yes, ma'am," he said again; added, "thank you, ma'am;" grabbed his pack and headed for the showers.

• • • •

THERE WAS SPACE FOR him at the counter at Bob's. He told the counterman he worked for Phyllis, and pretty quick a hamburg platter and a big Coke landed in front of him. He ate it all, even the lettuce, and was finishing up his Coke when he noticed somebody at his elbow.

Well, the place was packed, and it was probable somebody wanted his seat. Moss swallowed the last of his Coke and stood up.

"Sorry," he said—and right then recognized Felsic.

"Evenin'," Felsic said. "You have a good day at work?"

"I did. I like it. Boss said I can come back tomorrow."

"Phyllis likes an eager worker. You keep eager, and she'll keep happy. You mind if I walk a ways with you?"

Moss hesitated, looking at Felsic. He didn't get the feeling that this was a set-up, but . . .

"Just a walk down the beach," Felsic said, nice and easy. "I'll keep m'hands in m'pockets."

It came to Moss that he liked Felsic, and there wasn't really no harm going for a walk.

"Sure," he said.

• • • •

"YOU GOT A PLACE TO stay?"

That was a dangerous question, even if he *did* like Felsic. He wanted to stay here, in Archers Beach. Might be he was tired; he'd pushed himself hard the last couple days, and it could be his heart was tired. He'd think that, 'cept he didn't feel tired at all.

He felt more alive than he'd ever had, in all his life.

"I don't got a place, right yet," he said, not wanting to outright lie.

"That's all right," Felsic said. "The land hereabouts is welcoming. You just find someplace comfortable and set down roots, if you've a mind to."

Moss considered that as they walked up the beach. The sand strip was much skinnier now, the sound of the waves striking a constant thunder in his ears. His bones shook with it.

Sally had told him that the water changed—the tide came in and the tide went out, but he hadn't been, in any way, prepared for the reality of high tide. The thunder and the spray and the salt and the wind—all of it just made him feel like shouting and dancing and taking the thunder into his bones . . .

He closed his eyes and made himself pay attention to what Felsic had said.

"Just any place at all?" he asked. "Right here on the beach?"

"That could be a problem," Felsic said; "Generally the beach's held to be neutral—not belonging to the sea or the land, if you understand me."

Moss nodded. "No man's land."

There was a small silence, then Felsic outright laughed.

"That's it, that's it, exact! No man's land! You go a couple blocks inland, you might find something that'll do. Otherways, there's a youth hostel up at the top of Walnut. They'll spot you a night, you tell 'em you're working for Phyllis."

"Thanks," Moss said.

"No trouble, no trouble at all. I get off here." Felsic nodded toward the board walk crossing the dunes back onto the streets.

"I'll come with you, if I can," Moss said.

"Nothing stopping you that I see," Felsic answered easily, and so they crossed the boards together, and together they walked down to Grand, where Felsic turned right. Since he didn't have any reason to go left or right, Moss stayed with Felsic. There was something . . . not *kind*—No, thought Moss, definitely *not* kind—about Felsic. Comforting. Down to earth, that was it.

Moss decided that he liked Felsic very much, indeed.

They walked for two blocks, then Felsic angled across the street to a place that was nothing but two houses, backing on what smelled like a salt marsh.

"This is me," Felsic said, and reached out to touch him, softly, on the arm.

"Try for something further in. Don't wanna walk too far to work."

That made sense, Moss thought, and in the time it took him to think so, Felsic had walked around the back of one of the houses—and was gone.

Moss shivered, though it was plenty warm.

Just went in the back door, he told himself, and as if to bear him out, a light came on in the nearest house.

Moss nodded, shifted his pack on his back and turned back toward the heart of town.

• • • •

HE DIDN'T MUCH CARE for the idea of staying at anything called a "youth hostel." There were a number of bad things that routinely happened in dormitories, a couple of which he'd experienced up close and personal. The worst part of those being that he'd known better.

Well, it wasn't raining fit to drown a frog tonight. Tonight it was fine and clear, and there weren't too many people around, down this part of town. No reason for people to come down this way, which didn't offer no music, nor beer, nor nothing much at all, 'cept some little houses, like where Felsic lived. Back one street, there were trees and marsh.

He hit the corner and paused. From the left, he heard the crash and thunder of the waves against the shore. His feet turned, just slightly in that direction, and then—

It smelled like green leaves, and clean dirt, and pine, with a sweet underneath—maybe some flower he didn't know. From his right, away from the sea, borne on a breeze, was what he thought, but the wind was coming from the left, damp and fresh off the back of the waves.

Moss breathed in, letting the sweet, green air melt in his mouth like ice cream. He thought of laying himself down on a mound of pine needles, and sleeping safe and unmolested.

He turned right, away from the crash and boom of the ocean, following the promise as much as the scent. A couple feet down, he left the sidewalk, following a thin, faintly glowing trail, through weeds and reeds, past some sapling trees, between a green-glowing boulder and a white birch tree . . .

. . . and into a clearing floored with soft pine needles. Just off center of the clearing stood the remains of a big old tree, its limbs broken, but its trunk intact. He saw the small wrinkled objects dangling from one of the partial low branches, and put a name, at last, to the sweet smell.

Apples.

He sighed, looked around, feeling the welcome come up from the ground through the soles of his feet, and tears came to his eyes, even as he thought that this was what Felsic must've meant, about the land being welcoming.

And this little piece of land, right here, welcomed *him*.

"Thank you," he said, not feeling the littlest bit silly about talking out loud to trees and stones. "I'd like to stay here. I gotta get up in time for breakfast and work tomorrow, but I'll stay here, if you'll have me."

He looked around, and saw the gleam of one of those stupid pull-tabs among the pine needles.

"I'll clean up," he said, "and do what else needs done."

The scent of apples grew momentarily stronger; he yawned, hard on it, and slipped his pack off his back.

"It's been a long day," he told the trees, and cast about him. There was a soft mound of leaves and old needles just under the old apple tree, and it came to him that there would be a comfortable bed.

He settled in with a sigh, his pack under his head, pine needles and dead leaves for a blanket, and drifted off to sleep.

• • • •

HE WOKE TO BIRD SONG; opened his eyes and just laid there, smiling up into the broken branches above him and just feeling . . . happy. He'd had a dream that he'd talked to the grandmother of this little place, and she had told him that she loved him, and he could stay here forever, if he chose it.

Forever. Now, wasn't that something?

Moss sighed, and the bird sang again, louder this time, or so it seemed to Moss, and he remembered that he had to get up and go to work.

He left his pack leaning against the trunk of the old apple tree, confident that no one would mess with it while he was gone, then left his welcoming little piece of land, and headed down to Bob's for breakfast.

• • • •

HE WAS AT NOAH'S ARK well before the ten o'clock opening. Felsic was already there, tending the mules at the Coal Mine. Moss went over to help.

"Sleep good, deah?" Moss smiled.

"Best in years. Found a . . . welcoming spot."

"Did you now?" Felsic murmured, moving a brush slowly down a mule's short neck.

Moss braced himself, but Felsic didn't ask him where he was sleeping. They finished up combing and harnessing in companionable silence, broken at last by the clang of the side gate closing.

"That'll be Sally," Felsic said. "Best you learn set-up over at the slide. 'preciate the help, here; you got a good hand with the animals."

"My grampaw had mules at his place. I used to help with 'em."

"Well, he taught you good. Go 'long, now."

• • • •

IT WAS GOOD TO BELONG, it was good to work, and to earn money, and to have a good, safe place that was his to care for, and that cared for him back. Summer heated up, people kept on coming down to Archers Beach, 'til there wasn't hardly any room to walk on the sidewalks, and the rides were busy from opening to close. On July Fourth, him and Sally, and Felsic and Phyllis all climbed up to the top of Jack 'n Jill and stood on the platform to watch the fireworks. They were so high up, it was like being inside the sparks, and Moss felt each explosion echo in his chest.

In between, he worked on his land, clearing out the old trash, and finding the boundaries of the place that welcomed him, in particular, and bloomed under his care.

He met a bunch of folk, who worked on the rides, and elsewhere 'round the Beach. In particular, he met Vornflee, who was a friend of Felsic's, and who worked at the Moon Ride; and Bonny, who ran the carousel on the other side of the parking lot. Bonny was an important lady, Moss could see that. Even Phyllis deferred to her. She considered him for a long time after they was introduced, face serious; then she nodded, and put a hand on his shoulder.

"You'll do fine," she told him. "Just remember not to be afraid."

Truth said, he didn't have time to be afraid, busy as he was, and it was only 'cause Sally said something about the moon landing coming right up that he realized a month and more had gone past and he'd never been happier in his life.

"I'm goin' up to the top of the slide tonight, and see if I can't see it."

"See what?" Moss asked. "Moon's only just past new."

"The spaceship," Sally told him, with that little sniff that meant she was annoyed.

"Oh," Moss said, 'cause he didn't like Sally to be mad with him; "the spaceship. That's a different proposition. Maybe you *can* see that."

"I'm gonna try it," Sally said, determinedly; and added, with a side-look at him. "You can come up, too, if you want."

"Sure," he said. "Meet after dinner?"

She nodded, and the gong went off, and it was time to get to work.

• • • •

HE WAS FINISHING UP his clam chowder when he heard the first siren, and lifted his head, eyes wide.

"Engine number one," Vornflee said, tipping his head, burger held between two hands.

"Headin' down the hill," Felsic said, pushing back from the table, and standing. "Let me just step outside an—"

"Fire at the White Way!" Bob yelled, coming out from the kitchen. "Just heard it on the scanner! All call men wanted!"

Chairs scraped, and people jumped up, heading towards the door in a rush. Felsic started that way, too.

"You ain't a call man," Vornflee said.

"Fire at the White Way," Felsic said. "I better see to the mules."

Moss stood, too.

"I'll help," he said.

Vornflee sighed, put his burger down on the plate and got up, too.

"I'll watch."

• • • •

THERE WAS A PUMPER engine 'round back of the White Way, and two volunteer firemen using hoses on a small, smoky fire at the back corner. Moss followed Felsic 'round and over the fence, which was a quicker route to the Mine—and 'sides none of them had the key to the gate.

The space between the rides was filled with smoke, and Moss could hear the mules calling.

"Open the gate," Felsic told Vornflee. "Moss 'n me'll get the animals."

Vornflee nodded and ran; Moss followed Felsic.

The smoke was thicker by the entrance to the Mine, swirling around like it knew there was live things inside for it to torment. Felsic opened the door to the mule pen.

"Get the old man," Felsic said, and Moss grabbed a halter from the wall and went over the fence. The mules were anxious. A couple of the youngers brayed, pressed against the back of the enclosure, like they were trying to get away from the smoke that stalked them even there.

Old Man, though, he saw Moss and moved forward, two more mules following. Moss got the halter on, and patted the old mule.

"Let's go. s'only smoke so far, but you keep sensible, in case you see any fire." He looked at the two keeping pace, though they had no halters: Lacey and Gretel, both sensible folk.

"C'mon, then," he said, and walked them out of the enclosure, into the waiting area, and out into the park.

The smoke was still swirling, and Moss coughed as it got into his mouth. The Old Man was coming right along and his friends, too. Ahead, through the smoke, Moss could see the park gate open, and the parking lot full of cars beyond. He could hear music from the Pier, and people shouting.

Bonny from the carousel was waiting outside, with Phyllis. Bonny took Old Man's halter and led him away, toward the beach, Gretel and Lacy still following. Moss turned back, and here came Felsic, the rest of the mules following behind.

"Beach," said Phyllis, and Felsic turned that way.

An explosion rocked the night; smoke belched out of everywhere, like the sidewalks had opened up and hell was coming forth.

"Pull back, pull back! She's going up!"—that was the guys in the pumper truck, and there were other guys yelling—"Get those cars outta here!" and the sound of breaking glass, and—"Oh, no," Phyllis whispered. "Sally."

Moss spun, staring up, and there, silhouetted against the rising flames, Sally stood on the topmost platform of the giant slide, looking out over the confusion, illuminated and then cast into shadow by the dancing flames.

The fire was everywhere, now. The pile of sawdust at the bottom of the slide was afire. The Moon Ride was hidden in smoke, and long threads of flame licked out of the entrance into Noah's Ark.

Moss threw himself at the scaffolding, starting to climb.

"Sally!" he yelled.

"Moss!"

"Climb down!"

"The slide!" she shouted.

"The sawdust is on fire! Climb down!"

His chest was burning, which wasn't a surprise, with everything else on fire. He hung onto the scaffolding and looked up. Sally was climbing down. That was good. Sally climbed like a cat; he didn't worry about her falling, but if the scaffold got too hot to hold . . .

"Hey, you kids! Get outta there! Charlie! We need the hose!"

Water began to fall though the cloud of smoke. Moss clung and coughed, and watched Sally climb closer, and finally come to rest next to him.

"Why are they spraying us with water?"

"To keep the fire off of us," Moss gasped. "C'mon, we gotta get outta here."

• • • •

IT WAS GONE.

They'd stood there, all together, their arms around each others' waists, watching the amusement park burn.

Around ten o'clock Noah's Ark screamed like a live thing, foundered and collapsed in on itself, flames shooting out of the crater left behind.

Soon after, Jack 'n Jill, girders and slide all soft and black, sagged, crashed to its knees, and tipped over onto its side. The Moon Ride was gone by then, and the White Way was nothing more than ash and glowing timbers.

More fire trucks had arrived from the towns nearby, and they mostly concentrated on keeping the fire from reaching the Pier. They ran hoses into the sea, sprayed down the charred entrance ramp, and managed to keep the fire on land. There were people on the Pier, stranded for now, though Moss thought they'd be able to get off fine—tomorrow, maybe, after they'd gotten boats in and the last of the fire had died.

For now, he was tired. His chest ached, a little, his throat was raw, and his eyes streaming. At last somebody—maybe it was Bonny, maybe it was Phyllis—got them moving, away from the destruction, down Grand Avenue, to Bob's.

The place was jammed, even more than usual, no place to sit, and Moss finally sort of leaned up against the wall, feeling empty and sad. It was so crowded, it was hard to breathe, and his head was thumping hard, in an irregular rhythm that was making him sick to his stomach.

Air, that was what he needed. No, more than that. He needed to go back to his place, his little piece o'land, and sit down under the broken apple tree. Maybe take a nap . . .

He pushed away from the wall, but—funny thing; his knees just wouldn't hold him and down he went, hitting a chair and making a big noise, an even bigger noise than what was happening in his head, and—

"Moss!"

Felsic, that was; Felsic picking him up and holding him like he didn't weigh nothing at all.

"Gotta get home," he said—or tried to say—"I don't feel so good."

"Where's home, Mossie?" That wasn't Felsic, that was Bonny, and it was Bonny's hand, he thought, that came cool across his forehead.

"Down on Walnut, little place, old apple tree . . ."

"*That* place?" Phyllis sounded startled, but from a long, long ways away. He was so tired . . .

"Easy, easy . . ." Felsic murmured.

He felt a little jolt of cool peacefulness, and things come nearer again, though there was something funny happening with his eyes.

"Boy's accepted," Vornflee said, and Bob's voice came in over that, with—

"The kid's dying, Bonny . . ."

"Perhaps not," Bonny said. "Felsic?"

"I'll carry him." He felt himself lifted and shifted and put his head against something firm and soft.

"You stick with me," Felsic whispered in his ear, or maybe straight into his head. "Stick with me, Mossie; I'll get you home."

• • • •

MIGHT'VE BEEN HE BLACKED out, 'cause the next thing he did know was the welcome of his own place, rising up into him. He smiled, and he was so *very* tired . . .

"Moshe, listen to me." That was Bonny again, calling him by his right name, which he'd rather she didn't. He was Moss now, and he belonged to this place.

"That's right," Felsic said. "But you gotta choose it, brother. The land won't take—you gotta give."

"Dying," Moss said, remembering Bob, and his heart, and his promise to his Momma, that he'd be careful—but he had been careful, just not. . . careful enough.

"Dying," Felsic said; "but not dead. If you choose it, the land will have you. But not even the land can cure the dead."

"Moss—" Bonny again. "Open yourself up to the land. It knows you, this land; it loves you. Give yourself to it. I'll tell you; I knew the lady who lived in that apple tree; I was only a sapling myself when she bent down to disease, but I remember her. She was a stickler, and she didn't love easy, but once she did, her heart never closed. If what's left of her in this land chose you, then you can't do any better."

"How . . ." The thumping, and his breathing . . .

"Felsic," Phyllis said. "Let him go. It's his choice now, and you've kept him overlong, if his choice is to go."

Go? But he never wanted to go! He wanted to stay right here, here with this sweet place that loved him and kept him safe—that he loved and would shield with his life and more—he'd promised!

"And I promised," said a voice that he knew better than his own.

He opened his eyes, and there she was, the grandmother of this place.

She opened her arms, and he walked into her embrace.

He felt the welcome rise in him like the tide; he smelled fresh green leaves and sweet apples, pine, and leaf mold, and it seemed, for a minute, that his heart stopped beating altogether, and he didn't need breath at all. He felt the weight of the apple tree; knew the flowers like they were his own fingers, and the stones like they were his toes. He was Moss; he was the lady of the apple tree; and the little brown bird—the skylark—that sung him awake every morning, so he'd be on time for work. He was all of the pieces, and the perfect sum of everything . . .

"Here he comes back to us," Felsic said.

Moss opened his eyes, and smiled; feeling his land smile through him.

"I'm not going to die," he said, like he was comforting Felsic.

"Not for a good, long while, I'm thinking," Felsic answered, and all around him he heard an exhale as if a roomful of folk had suddenly sighed at once in relief and pleasure.

"Are we all . . . like this?" he asked, looking from face to face around him.

"We all have taken service with the land," Bonny said briskly. "Each in our own way."

"'cept Sally," said Vornflee.

"Sally's a cat," Moss said. "Even I know that."

"That's right," Felsic said. "Now, how're you feeling, brother Moss?"

Moss laughed, and sat up, full of energy and delight. He felt a chipmunk run light over the land, pine cone in his mouth, and grinned.

"Thank you," he said, to all of them gathered, and those others, who were listening in through their own connection to a piece of land, or a slice of marsh, or a rock, or a tree. He could . . . almost . . . see them all, behind his eyes. Soon, he'd sort them out.

"You okay with this, Moss?" Felsic asked him, and Moss laughed again.

"I'm home," he said; "and I ain't never leaving. Hard to be any more okay than that."

Will-o'-the-wisp

F elsic hadn't ever thought of herself as a coward—well. She hadn't ever thought she was brave, neither. You just did what there was to do, taking the good with the bad, like they say, and letting the sea sort it out.

That sort of thinking, now; that worked just fine for marshes and wetlands, and rivers, too, for all Felsic knew about it. Nothing so fine as a river, Felsic; just a little patch o'salt marsh, that was all. Not much to look at, and likely to smell like wet mud and rottin' reeds at low tide, but it did for her.

More than did, until just lately, when the Enterprise took a sudden interest in her, and Kate Archer no help at all.

She opened up her drawer in the dresser—and didn't that beat everything, her having a dresser drawer full of rolled socks and underclothes, and t-shirts. She'd even gone down to Dynamite and gotten herself some party clothes for tomorrow night's dance—those were in the closet. Bright red shirt, a long vest embroidered with blue, and red, and yellow flowers, and a pair of tight black trousers. Peggy'd make a face at all that color. Peggy'd be in black, like usual, but Felsic liked colors. Some folks, they said there wasn't nothin' like color in a salt marsh, but, then, some folk couldn't see past the end of their noses—not that Felsic held it against 'em. You were born blind, or you were born Sighted, and there wasn't no sense blaming either kind for being who they were.

Peggy, now, she was Sighted, and there was the problem, right there. If she hadn't been—well.

No sense dwelling on that, neither. If Peggy'd been blind-born, then she'd never seen anything other than what Felsic had wanted to her see, and the Season would've got done, and she'd gone on back down into the Flatlands—New Jersey, in particular—and Felsic'd gone back to winter with her little bit of marsh.

No dresser drawers in *that* might-be, nor party clothes, nor spooning in a tall bed, under a quilted blanket . . . leastways, not with the Season over. Felsic'd had her some good times, never you doubt it, and there wasn't no reason she couldn't've had a fine old time with Peggy Marr, and vice-versa, 'til it got time for her to go.

Except Peggy, now. Peggy'd turned out to be . . . different.

She'd never lied to Peggy. Peggy didn't hold with lying; you saw that first thing. It was just Felsic's good luck that Peggy'd never asked what it was she was, or where'd she'd lived before they'd set up house in this snug little condo, and bought all new kitchen stuff, and a sofa, and a TV set.

And that was because Peggy thought Felsic was another Kate Archer—that being her role model for people who walked off the edge of the sidewalk—just maybe without the material advantages that came with being an Archer of Archers Beach. In fact, Peggy *might've* thought that Felsic'd been rooming with Vornflee and Moss . . . an' it could just be Felsic'd given her suppositions a gentle nudge in that direction.

Wasn't lying, exactly, to let somebody have suppositions.

This now, though. She was close to a line, here, and the fact of the matter was that either side she chose, there was a lie waiting for her.

She pulled the manila envelope out from under her t-shirts, and crossed over to the bed. Lifted the flap like the thing was like to bite her, which it hadn't done the last three times she'd had it open, and wasn't like to do now.

Inside—they were simple things. Everyday things, like mundane folk carried 'round with them in their wallets, or set aside in a file drawer and hardly thought on 'em again.

Driver's license.

Social Security card.

Birth certificate.

Every single one of 'em genuine, though Felsic was pretty sure she didn't know how to drive, and the only thing she remembered being present at her birth, backaways, was a momma mallard with a knowing button eye, who'd winked at her, then gone tail-up in the water, in search of a little something to eat.

And that there was going to be the hardest thing to explain to Peggy. Kate Archer was . . . human.

Felsic was *trenvay*, born out of the needs and desires of a particular bit of geography. Felsic happened to be . . . call it the *personification* of a little tiny corner of Scarborough Marsh, that the locals called Bufflehead Cove. Why she'd arisen—well, that was a mystery, even to Felsic. But, having gotten herself born, in the way that *trenvay* are, she'd set about the care and keeping of her bit of marsh. That'd been enough, just at first, when she'd been young and simple. But as she'd gotten older, and stronger, her horizons had widened, in a manner of speaking. That just naturally came with age, so far as Felsic'd seen. Why, Kate Archer's Gran'd been born a dryad, and tied tight to her tree. And now she had some years on her, didn't she just wander all over town? So, Felsic'd begun to take an interest, which she had to, the Beach having been without a proper Guardian for so long—and the result of all her care and effort being—

A driver's license, a birth certificate, a Social Security card . . .

. . . and a proper name.

Francis Eleanor Sicot, so it said on the paper, born to one Willow Jane Sicot, no father listed, at the South Portland Medical Center, about thirty years ago, which put her near enough to Peggy's age. On paper, leastways.

Lies, every bit of it, even if there'd ever been a Willow Jane Sicot, who'd gone and got herself in trouble. It was in her to wonder where was Willow Jane now, and if maybe she might need a hand—and she shook herself, hard.

There was a brisk tap on the door. She snatched up the papers, like she was going to hide them again—then let them fall back onto the bed. Past time for hiding, she told herself sternly; you're almost into lying.

"Felsic?" Peggy's voice came through the door. "You OK?"

She took a deep breath, looked down, and turned toward the door.

"Almost," she said, wryly, and feeling her stomach grab up into a knot.

"Whyn't you come on in, Peg? There's some things you gotta know."

• • • •

"SO YOU'RE TELLING ME that these papers here are—counterfeit? That somebody here in town made them?"

Peggy shook her head and put the Social Security card down on the bedspread next to the other papers.

"Damn, I wish I'd know about this back at the beginning of the Season. I wouldn't have had to play quite so many games with Arbitrary and Cruel's hiring policies."

"You'd've ordered in false IDs for the whole crew?" Felsic asked, momentarily diverted.

"You're thinking it would've been expensive? I had an expense account and total discretion. By the time they did the audit, the Season would've been over." She looked thoughtful, lips pursed.

"More or less the same result, actually," she said, and shrugged. "So, Felsic, if these papers are—counterfeit . . . I guess I'd like to know why you need counterfeit papers?"

"That's a good question. Kate's of the opinion that I'm on the edge of getting more responsibility on the Beach. The kind of responsibility that needs a Social Security card to be listened to."

"*Kate* gave you these?"

Her tone said she didn't believe it, and Felsic didn't blame her. Truth said, Kate'd looked as horrified as Felsic, when she'd opened up the envelope. 'course, Kate had some idea of how unsettling the Enterprise was, just as a general concept, which Peggy didn't.

"Kate offered to talk to you about how them papers come in," she said. "I don't understand it, myself—not that I think Kate does. Her edge over us is she's seen it done more'n once."

Peggy nodded.

"I'll keep it in mind," she said slowly, and reached out to tap the birth certificate.

"But if this is counterfeit—who are you really?"

Well, now, that was the question, wasn't it?

Felsic took a hard breath, feeling chill all the way up from the bottom of her feet to the top of her head.

Peggy . . . There was some things even the Sighted shouldn't ought to see, and the first . . .

"Felsic," she said, quietly. "You know I won't get mad, so long as you tell me the truth."

Mad, no. But there was plenty of room for horror, and other kinds of upset that she'd never willingly bring Peggy to feel.

Shoulda been smarter, Felsic told herself, but there wasn't any way to go back to the first of the Season, and seein' her for the first time, and feeling that tug that meant here was a prize worth having . . .

"You promise me something," she said suddenly, and knew by the change on Peggy's face that her voice had been every bit as harsh as she'd feared.

"What's that?"

"You promise me, if you need to leave—to leave this house, on account of what truth I'll be showing you. If you need to leave here, you'll go to Kate Archer, and tell 'er."

Peggy frowned. "Tell her what?"

"You'll know what, if you gotta say it out," Felsic said with certainty, and looked down at the documents spread over their bed. She used her chin to point at the driver's license.

"That right there's your first lie," she said. "That photograph. I don't—the real me ain't quite so . . . smooth."

She turned to the chest of drawers, facing the mirror there. Peggy'd see the reflection over her shoulder. She didn't stop to wonder why she thought that might be less upsetting than seeing it straight.

There was a face in the mirror—an easy, comfortable face that she wore for those who didn't believe in magic, or creatures of the night, or spirits of the place. That face was glamour, and that's *all* it was. Sugar-coating, if you like it that way.

Her real face . . . well, she'd been born out of the will of a piece of marshland, now hadn't she? Marsh had the general shape of things, but it'd been a little foggy on details.

That being so, her real face was what you might call rugged: broad and flat; nose not much more'n a bump; no chin to speak of;

and a wide, thin-lipped mouth. Her eyes were deep, and dark; the rest of her shape following the broad, flat design.

She took a breath, staring into her own eyes, and breathed out, releasing the glamour, part of her waiting for Peggy to scream.

Except that the face in the mirror didn't change. It remained obstinately round, with an adorable up-tilted nose, generous mouth, and a sturdy chin. Only the eyes were as they should be—dark as bog water, with glimmers of cinnamon in the depths. Her shape was strong; broad in the shoulders, and sturdy at the waist; and the t-shirt clung somewhat to definite breasts.

Felsic felt a little stutter of horror all her own. Behind her, she heard the bedclothes shift, then Peggy was behind her in the mirror, arms around her waist.

"Hey, nobody's license photo is any good," she said. "You should see mine. No, on second thought, you shouldn't. I don't want to scare you."

Felsic leaned back into Peggy's hug, and tried to think.

The Enterprise was powerful, and unpredictable; everybody knew that—*trenvay* and townie alike. You didn't ask, that was it, and if you were lucky, the Enterprise didn't answer, anyway.

But it had taken an interest in her, and somehow, by. . .taking delivery of those papers, she'd gotten . . . nailed into place. Woven into the warp and woof of the mundane world; her aspect fixed—

And her duty? Her little bit of marsh, that was her life, and her reason for being born?

"Felsic?"

"Peg, I'm not . . . like you," she said.

"Right, you're like Kate—which is to say that you're an extra-special person with powers of which I wot not. I don't mean to imply that you and Kate are interchangeable. For one thing, she's straight."

And it had used to be that Felsic was neither one kind nor another, pleasure being pleasure, and the marsh not expecting to deliver or sire children. Didn't seem any way to exactly explain that, either. Felsic bent her head, stomach cramped and unhappy. She put her hands over Peggy's where they were caught together at her waist, and squeezed.

"You're upset," Peggy said quietly. "What else do you need to tell me?"

Felsic swallowed.

Papers, she thought. She had papers, now, and the papers trapped her in a lie—except, what had Kate said? That the papers brought *additional* duty. Her primary duty, that was still with her. She wasn't mundane, not wholly. What those papers made her was—a little more visible to those who were generally blind.

That was all right. Well. With work, and some help from the Guardian of Archers Beach, it could be made to be all right. But that—*them*. Those half-blind folk, *they* weren't where her heart was. Peggy . . .

Peggy not only wanted the truth; she *needed* to have the truth.

Felsic shivered. Other *trenvay* knew where to find her—where to find *her soul*, she guessed the marsh must be, which was a funny old thought, and not one she remembered having before. The Guardian surely knew where to find her. But, she'd never shown herself—her soul—to anyone . . . mundane. Never, in all the winters she'd been alive.

"Show you," she said hoarsely.

"What?"

Felsic cleared her throat.

"There's a thing I gotta show you," she said, and lifted her head, catching Peggy's eyes in the mirror.

"Right now, before I lose my nerve."

• • • •

"HERE."

"Here?"

They were holding hands, standing side-by-side on a piece of marsh that, to Peggy's eyes, Felsic figured, looked pretty much like every other piece of marsh they'd walked through to get to this one spot, where Felsic's blood jumped with joy, and of a sudden she was wide, and deep; and slow and secret. Grasses tickled her ribs, and crabs scuttled along her skin; she felt a harrier land on a bush just over there, heard the scream of a frog pierced by a heron . . .

"Tell me about it," Peggy said quietly.

Felsic blinked at her.

"Don't know there's much to tell," she said, and her voice was slow, and deeper, too, like the voice of the dark waters all around. "I can name off the plants, if you like it, or—"

"Tell me what you're feeling," Peggy said.

So Felsic told her about the tickling salt hay, and the hurrying crabs, the slow fish, the intensity of the hunting heron, and the hawk fair sitting on her shoulder. They moved along, still hand-in-hand, Felsic making sure the mud supported Peggy, while she showed her where, come spring, there'd be aster, and bayberry; wild orchid and blueberries . . .

"We're getting ready for the long sleep," she said. "Hay's starting to die back, like you see. Pretty soon now the visitor birds'll be leaving; the muskrats an' all that sort'll be settling into dens. Not so much for a *trenvay* to do, 'cept keep good watch, an' be sure nobody with his brains in his pants comes through here with a snow machine, or, worse, a four-wheeler.

"Old days, first snow, I'd just settle in to sleep myself. Some still do. Others of us, we come to keep more active watch in the winter. There's more things can go wrong lately, and they just don't happen in the warm days."

She heard those last words, and came to the realization that she'd been talking along, heedless, for . . . quite some while, telling Peggy all about it, like she'd asked.

Stomach clenched, she turned and looked down into violet eyes, which were looking steadfastly up into her face.

Felsic thought she might ought to say something—and then thought that she'd already said more'n enough.

She swallowed.

Peggy smiled and reached up to touch her cheek. "I love you," she said.

• • • •

"SO, WHO'S WILLOW JANE Sicot?" Peggy asked. It was a couple days after their walk in the marsh, and the end-of-Season party. They were sitting at the bar in their kitchen, sharing a third cup of coffee.

It took Felsic a tick to recall the name; then she shrugged.

"Something the Enterprise snatched outta the wind, I'm guessing. Person with a driver's license and a Social, she's gotta at least have had a mother."

Peggy frowned.

"Kate seemed to think that the Enterprise—or whoever writes out those papers and *sends them in*—works within reality. It might've gotten away with making up a mother, before computerized record-keeping and all our—" She made quote marks in the air—"*modern day improvements*", but not anymore. I'm betting there is—or at least *was*—a Willow Jane."

"Could be," Felsic said. "Don't see that it has much of anything to do with me."

"Do you mind if I look around?" Peggy asked. "I'm curious."

Felsic grinned.

"You ain't got enough to do with getting Fun Country in shape to open in April?"

Peggy opened her eyes wide.

"What, that? That's a piece of cake, and I could eat it in my sleep. This thing with your mom—that's *interesting*."

"*My mom*, is it?" Felsic shook her head, between amusement and concern. "Peggy, you know—"

Peggy held up a hand.

"I know, I know. Born of the marsh in service of the marsh. Not even technically human. You said it. Kate said it. You're the experts. But—I'm still curious. You don't mind?"

"No . . ." said Felsic, and told herself that she didn't.

• • • •

"TURN RIGHT HERE," PEGGY said.

Felsic obediently slowed the Prius, put on the right turn signal, and made a slow, careful turn into a skinny driveway near overgrown with box cedar. She steered the car carefully—she'd been practicing daily, sometimes with Peggy, other times with Kate, and on one occasion with Cap'n Borgan himself, who'd actually managed to squeeze his big self into the Prius' front seat.

Despite all that practice, she still wasn't best friends with the idea of driving a car, and if left to herself, she'd rather walk anywhere she needed to go.

This, now; this was supposed to've been a practice drive, out Route 9 to 1, but it seemed like Peggy'd changed her mind.

The drive opened up into a little half-moon parking lot, with lines marking spaces for eight cars; three had cars in them.

Facing the parking lot was a low building with faded blue shingles, and a sign over the double glass doors.

"*Maison de la mer*?" Felsic said. "What're we needing at the House of the Sea, Peg?"

"Jane W. Sicot lives here," Peggy said, and when Felsic didn't say anything back right away, on account of having to sort through why the name was important, she added, "Your mother."

"Thought my mother was Willow Jane Sicot." Felsic was on firm ground, now. "And only on a piece of paper, at that."

"People change their names around. Turns out that Jane W. is Jane Willow; she confirmed that when I spoke to her on the phone. Willow's a family name."

"You talked to her on the phone?" Felsic repeated, feeling her stomach clench up tight.

Peggy looked at her, straight and stern.

"You said you didn't mind if I tried to find her."

"And nor yet, I don't. I don't recall ever being asked, *did I want to meet her* if you did find her."

There was a small silence.

"That's fair," Peggy said; "we didn't discuss that. Would you like to meet Jane W. Sicot, Felsic?" She looked around at the mostly empty parking lot, the battered building in need of paint, and the sign over the double doors.

"It doesn't look like anybody here gets a lot of company."

• • • •

THE ROOM WAS EMPTY, except for the lone figure in the wheelchair overlooking the autumn marsh, and a bunch of metal chairs, folded up and leaning against the wall.

"She's always here," the nurse said in an undertone. "The night nurse says some shifts she comes through and there she is, in the window, and there can't be anything to see at night! I mean, look at it! There's hardly anything to see in broad daytime!"

Peggy squeezed Felsic's hand gently. Neither one answered the nurse, though Felsic thought the woman in the chair showed good sense. Who *wouldn't* prefer a view of the marsh to the various activity rooms they'd passed on the way from the front of the building to the back?

"Jane?" the nurse said brightly. "You have visitors!"

The figure did not turn from her contemplation of the marsh. Felsic approved. Who were they, anyways, to interrupt her?

Peggy, though, had a different idea. She strode forward, pulling Felsic with her.

"Ms. Sicot, I'm Peggy Marr. I called you yesterday, and you said it would be all right for my friend and me to stop by today for a chat."

The figure turned the chair, slowly, pale October light falling across a ravaged pale face, and glittering in short white hair.

"That's right," she said, and her voice was fine and firm. "Pull up some chairs, and set a spell. Rachel," she said, apparently to the nurse; "thank you."

"Now, you know it's no trouble. Can I bring you anything? A blanket? It's chilly in here, isn't it?"

"I'm comfortable," said Ms. Sicot.

The nurse hesitated, then nodded and went away.

Peggy grabbed a folding chair, and Felsic did. They carried them back to the window and unfolded them, facing the woman in the wheelchair.

"Thank you for agreeing to see us, Ms. Sicot," Peggy said.

"It's not like I've got much else to do," the old woman said. "Call me Jane, please. Now, what's this about a daughter?"

Peggy extended a hand and touched Felsic on the sleeve. Ms.—Jane's eyes followed the motion.

"This is my partner, Francis Eleanor Sicot," Peggy said.

The white head inclined formally. "Francis."

"Friends call me Felsic, ma'am," she said easily, and leaned forward a little, looking like a *trenvay* looks, with something more than mundane seeing, and saw that the woman—this Jane—was old, and sick. Sick to death; Felsic saw it plain, and the time she had left less than a single hand of days.

Dying, and her preferred companion was nothing more or less than Scarborough Marsh.

"Felsic, then. You think you might be my daughter?"

"No, ma'am. Peggy thinks that. She's got a mother, see, and she just naturally don't want me to be without anything she finds good."

Peggy made a sound like a sneeze. Jane Sicot smiled.

"That's what love is; wanting good things for your better half. I assume you are the better half?"

"No'm, I'm nothing such. Peggy's the best of both of us."

Another sneeze, and Peggy's fingers pressed hard around her wrist.

The smile widened, then faded.

"What I'm thinking," Felsic continued; "and I hope you'll excuse me, if I'm rude—what I'm thinking is you might be a little long in the years to be my mother. Birth certificate has the name as Willow Jane Sicot."

Jane Sicot tensed in her chair. It was the Marsh let Felsic feel how her heart stuttered, though why the Marsh would trouble itself...

"Willow Jane Sicot," Jane repeated, and sighed, her heartbeat more even now, though slow and tired. She smiled, though it wobbled 'round the edges.

"I don't think you're rude at all, Felsic—in fact, you're right. I am not young enough to be your mother." She took a breath.

"But I'm plenty old enough to be your grandmother."

• • • •

"WILLOW JANE . . . SHE was a good girl, not a mean bone in her body. She'd been born with—well, back then, they called it *mongolism*, and it wasn't expected that those who had it would live much past little children. Back then, they said, too, that the best place for such children was in an institution. Well! It don't take any great mind to connect the dots there, and I figured, if Willow wasn't to live long, she ought to be loved and looked after like any little child, in her own home, with her parents caring for her.

"So we brought her home. Our house was right on the edge of the Marsh. The mister, he fished, and I did the books for the 'change from my kitchen table, and I kept Willow right by me." She smiled, then, dreamy with memory.

"She was a happy baby, and I was certain I'd made the right decision, to bring her home, to be inside of her family, for as long as she had."

"Problem was, the mister didn't warm to Willow, despite she was his daughter. And finally of a day just after her fourth birthday, he said to me that she'd be better off in—a home, is what he called it. And, well, that was a choice, right there, and me—I chose Willow."

She leaned back in her chair and closed her eyes.

Felsic felt Peggy stir next to her.

"Mrs. Sicot, you don't have to—"

Jane Sicot opened her eyes.

"No, you're wrong there. I do have to. This has a point that concerns you, and—well, Peggy Marr, you were right to call me. There's not much story left, and I think all three of us'll be better for hearing it."

Peggy sighed.

"Felsic?"

"We asked," Felsic said, reaching out to take her hand. "Only polite to hear the answer."

"Thank you."

Another rest against the chair; another series of slit-eyed, shallow breaths.

"Come to it, Willow lived past childhood, she lived through being a teenager. There wasn't any question of sending her to school; I taught her what I could, at home. We still lived right there on the edge of the Marsh, and she wandered there, most days; never come to harm. I was still doing the books for the Fisherman's Exchange, and for some of the fishermen, too. Made enough for the two of us, and the neighbors helped keep the house in repair."

She paused.

This now, Felsic thought; *this* is the painful part, even worse than the mister left them, for cause of not being able to love his own daughter.

"One afternoon, she didn't come home, and I was so absorbed in unknotting Caleb Varney's quarterlies, that I didn't even miss her until it was full dark.

"I went out looking, and—and I found her, not far. Short of it, she'd been beaten, and raped, and just left there in the mud . . ."

Hard breath.

"Eight months later, there was a baby. By then, we had Social Services in it, like we'd never had, all the years before, with their clipboards, and their rules . . .

"It was the Social Service caseworker who told me that Willow's baby had died, not five minutes after the nurse came to tell me that Willow was gone, herself."

Jane Sicot shook her head.

"I believed her—Social Services—and it didn't strike me odd 'til later, that nobody'd brought that baby to me, so she could be buried with her mother. And when I asked, Social Services said the hospital had taken care of it; and the hospital referred me to Social Services . . ."

She met Felsic's eyes, hers damp.

"That's bothered me for a lot of years, now."

Felsic nodded.

"I can see it would."

"You got the look of her, a little, and if you got a birth certificate with her name on it—I guess they must've fostered you out?"

"I had good care," Felsic told her, gentle as she could, and mindful of Peggy, who knew the truth, and valued the telling of it.

"I was wanted, and I couldn't've asked for no better life than I've had."

Jane Sicot smiled.

"Good. That's good."

"I'm sorry," Peggy said softly.

Jane Sicot turned her head. She was smiling, slightly.

"Nothing to be sorry for, Peggy Marr. I'm glad you called, and I'm glad you brought her to me. Now, if you'll do me a favor, like I done you—I'd like a few minutes to talk to Felsic alone. If you wanna walk slow back to the front desk, and tell 'em I'm wantin' that blanket after all, and you'll bring it along to me, that'll be time enough."

"Felsic?" Peggy said. "You'll be all right?"

Why she wouldn't be all right alone with a woman too sick to raise her arm was more than Felsic could figure, but it was like Peggy to want to know she'd feel safe, and so she gave a smile, and a nod.

"I'll be fine, Peg."

"All righty, then. One blanket the slow way, coming up."

She rose and left them, walking briskly until she reached the hall, when her pace changed to a light-footed stroll, nothing like her usual businesslike stride.

Felsic grinned again, and turned back to Jane Sicot, who was looking at her closely.

"Willow used to tell me about her friends, in the Marsh," she said. "Pretty lights, and mist shaped like people that you could see right through, and otters who would come up and sun themselves on a rock and tell her a story. I thought—well, I thought it was made up, who wouldn't think that?"

Felsic didn't say anything.

"I thought that," Jane Sicot said, "until the night she didn't come home. I ran out into the Marsh—it was pitch, and there was more chance that I'd fall and break an ankle than there was of finding her. I called, though, and I wandered, and was prolly lost myself, when, up from the weeds come a glowing ball, all blue and gold and friendly seeming, and I know *you'll* believe me when I say that glowing ball led me straight to where he'd left her, bleeding and broken, and covered in mud. Took me straight there, and then lighted me back to the house. I looked back, when I got to the door, and it was there, like it was watching. I pushed the door open and it—blinked out."

Felsic nodded.

"This doesn't surprise you," said Jane Sicot.

"No, ma'am."

"Can you see these things, too? Like . . . your mother did?"

"I can see 'em, yes, ma'am." She paused, her eyes straying over the sick woman's shoulder to the marsh. Sat here all the time, did she? Even in the dark nighttime?

"You can see 'em, too, I think." She met the other woman's eyes, and got a slow nod.

"They give me drugs, you know. For the pain. I'm not really sure what I'm seeing, not always, but it's certain that whatever it or they are, they're not going to come in and talk with me."

Felsic nodded again.

"We're shy, some of us; others of us, we're young."

"Us?" repeated Jane. "You're magic, then, are you?"

"No'm; I'm the most natural thing there is, all us Marsh-folk are. We each take care of our own little bit o'business. Me, now, I'm Bufflehead Cove, right back from the Seagull in Archers Beach. Other thing you need to know is—I'm old. Way too old for you to've been my gran, nor your girl m'mother—though I wouldn't have minded if it'd gone that way."

Jane laughed, short and breathy.

"I don't think I would've minded, either."

She moved the fingers of her right hand, like she was asking Felsic to move closer.

"Tell me what it's like, being Bufflehead Cove."

She thought about that for a minute, remembering back to the day she'd taken Peggy into the Marsh. Then she leaned forward, took one wracked, cold hand between both of hers, looked into the dark, too-bright eyes, raised her glamour, and *showed* her.

It wasn't done, not usually; you didn't want to set a mundane running mad. But Jane Sicot was dying. It could've been that the drugs made it easier for her to See, or the dying itself.

Anywise, for a whole turn of seasons that lasted only four minutes by the mundane clock, Jane Sicot *was* Bufflehead Cove, every stone, every tiny green crab, every tall, stalking blue heron. She rose and fell in the sluggish, salty water, and the wind combed her salt hay hair. Sunlight beat down upon her, drying the mud, and she put forth blossoms, and blueberries, and felt the leaves peel away in the cold wind, while the hay withered, and the snow came down upon her, and she slept.

She slept.

Footsteps struck Felsic's ear. She sat back, still holding Jane's hand, and turned her head to watch Peggy come down the room, blanket over one arm.

"Is she . . ."

"Asleep, is all." Felsic laid the ravaged hand on a thin knee, and stood to help Peggy drape the blanket 'round her shoulders.

"Should we say good-bye?" Peggy asked.

"I'd say let her sleep," Felsic said, and she nodded.

They folded up the chairs, put them quietly back against the wall, and walked out of the building.

"What did she want to ask you?" Peggy said, when they'd gotten into the car.

"She'd caught sight of some of the marsh *trenvay*," Felsic said. "Wanted to know what it was like."

"And you told her?"

"I showed her. Figured it couldn't do any harm."

She turned suddenly in her seat.

"Peggy?"

"Yes?"

"Thank you," Felsic said. "I'm glad you brought me down here for this."

"Not mad?"

"Not even," said Felsic, and leaned forward.

"Love you," she said, and their kiss was all the magic she could ever need.

The Wolf's Bride

The dogs of the village knew him; and he passed without challenge from forest edge to market street, walking with a predator's sure, silent tread down the moss-lined way.

Above, the night-time sky was a velvet stole, across which a handful of jewels had been scattered, winking in bright hues of gold, and green, and blue. It was silent in the darkness, as it never was in the day, when the merrybells sang the sun's praises. His bones told him that it was mid-night, and he lengthened his stride, then breathed a laugh at his own foolishness.

He had meant to be earlier. Indeed, he had meant to arrive at the sun's height, with leisure to stop by his own small house to bathe and attire himself in what finery he possessed, so that he might come seemly before the headwoman.

Well, and now he had more than ample leisure to bathe and make himself fine, for the headwoman would surely not rise for some hours yet, and if he was wise—which he could be—he would allow her time to break the night's fast, and drink a bracing cup, or two, of thistle tea before he approached her with his topic.

Thus occupied with his thoughts, he came to the main square; the village cistern a squat shadow against the night's velvet; and the merrypole a dark lance driven upward toward the stars.

Another shape, lithe, hesitant, and faintly limned in green detached from the greater bulk of the cistern. Her scent traveled to him on the breeze, but she was fleeter yet, hesitation flung to the stars, as she raced silent across the mossy square. His bow was slung; all he need do was open his arms, and catch her as she flew into them.

"Cael!"

They were much of a height; she stood on her toes to grasp another few inches, and brought her mouth down on his.

Her kiss was a complex thing; demanding, angry, relieved; then nuance was lost as his blood heated and he returned her passion with his own.

"Ah!"

She pulled away first, settling onto flat feet, her hands on his shoulders, her gaze holding his, for she saw as sharply in the dark as in the day, did his Senaya; and he had a hound's keen vision.

"I looked for you earlier," she said; and, "I was worried."

"I had looked to arrive earlier," he answered; and, "Never worry, love."

"If you would stand away from desperate ventures, perhaps I would learn not to worry!"

That was merely the last flames of a fiery temper, ignited by her fear. Senaya was bold; fearless on her own behalf. For him, though, she feared, as if he still had his milk teeth.

"What happened?" she asked then; "to delay you?"

"An old ram charged a young shepherd, after the dogs had done. We were called back, to mend the line, and bring the runaways home."

She looked disbelieving, as well she might.

"The ram took four ewes with him; and the four ewes each took a lamb. They led us a dance. After, the master would have it that I had mismanaged the thing and thought to withhold a portion of my wage."

She stirred in his arms.

"Never mind; he thought better of it."

Senaya laughed.

"Yes, I expect he did—and quickly, too!"

Laughter lit her face, and this time it was he who kissed her.

"Well, then," he said, eventually, and just as if herding goats from my lord Aeronymous' honor to that of Lord Eredith was dangerous beyond reckoning...

"My last chancy venture is complete. Tomorrow, I will offer myself to the headwoman and to Seafort."

She relaxed against him and lay her head on his shoulder with a sigh.

"And we may be married."

Senaya was the headwoman's third daughter. Her gift was herbalism, and healing, which placed her high in the village's regard. He ... was not of the village, though he had lived within it all his life. His mother, no one knew; nor his father. His foster mother had been a ranger, and one day had brought him back from the forest, with a tale of having found him in a wolf's den, naked, and with gnawed bones all about him.

It had been his foster mother who held shy of giving him to the village. Best, she had told him, that he make that decision, when he was old enough to know himself.

Well. His foster mother had her own foibles, and there had been some old matter that lay between her and the headwoman. Some seasons back, she had married, herself, and chose to go to her spouse's village. He had been on his own by then, established in his own small house. He had helped her pack what few items she would take with her, and to unmake the house that had been hers. Together, they had sung the memories out of the ground, and sowed heartsease and blanc-mallow, to freshen it for the next to build there.

He might have offered himself to the village anytime after establishing his own residence, but there had been pride involved. He would not come as a pauper; and, when it came plain that Senaya returned his regard, he had determined to come to her as an equal, and not only as "the healer's chosen."

Pride was satisfied, now, and tomorrow all would be put to right. They had decided between them that their first act as bond-mates would be to take his house down and rebuild it as a part of hers, making the single dwelling, in truth, *their* house.

He sighed.

"Regrets?"

"That it is not tomorrow evening, perhaps. No others."

She laughed and stirred in his arms.

"Come," she said, standing back and catching his hand. "Let us see you to bed. For I will tell you plainly, my Cael, that, even should you miss the headwoman tomorrow day, you will in no way be safe from me, tomorrow night!"

"That seems no threat at all," he protested, allowing her to pull him across the square.

"You have not yet heard what I will do to you!" Senaya told him, and laughing, they skipped like children, under the stars.

· · · ·

THE HEADWOMAN WAS THE heart and the life of Seafort Village; she was the repository of the village's combined power; their defender and their solace. This was the natural order of things, that the weaker ceded their power to the strongest, who conserved it for everyone and wielded it when necessary.

Being a power, the headwoman glowed, even in the bright daylight, with the merrybells in full tongue. She glowed, and she frowned, and she continued to do both, even after he had said what was in his heart, and bowed to her honor. No word passed her lips, and he felt neither the thrill of her power passing through him, nor the ache of his, being drawn.

Perhaps, he thought, he had misdone the thing. Perhaps, she waited to learn if he was fully and wholly set upon this path.

Reasoning thus, he called his own meager power, shivering, though it rose hot, as always; breathed in to center himself before opening—

"Hold."

The word was spoken quietly; the headwoman rarely raised her voice. Rarely, too, did she speak a Word, unless it was truly needed. He did not think she spoke such now, though he felt a little sting, as if she had lashed his pride.

Straightening, he allowed his power to fall back to its nesting place at the base of his spine, and met the headwoman's emerald eyes full on.

She smiled, then, and nodded; for she had ever been one to admire boldness.

"You would have the thing done, and quickly," she said. "I understand your impatience. And yet I must ask you, Cael Sojourner, if you have thought this matter through." Her smile came again.

"With your head, understand me. I do not often advise others to discount Senaya, but I counsel you, if you find it possible, to set her to one side of your considerations."

He paused for three long breaths, that he not seem over-hasty in his reply, then made answer.

"Mother, I would have offered myself any time these last six seasons. I have lived here for all of my life that I recall. Who else would I come to, save the folk, and the place, that has sheltered me so long?"

"And yet you did not offer yourself until now," she said; "what held you away?"

He sighed.

"Pride. I would not come a beggar, with nothing, in fact, to give to the commonweal, save my weakness and my need."

"And now you stand before me possessed of a respectable store of power, and none may say that Cael took more than he gave. I understand. And yet, there is this matter of your . . . other attributes, which are warp and woof of Cael—power, surely! But not as we measure or know it."

"Mother, I—"

"Peace," she said mildly, and pointed at the stool near her feet. "Sit. My neck is cricked with staring up at you."

He sat, arranging his legs about the little stool, and gazed up into her face as fair and round as the moon.

"Your foster mother and I too often saw past each other, but in this instance, I agreed with her. You will recall that she did not give you to the village, but maintained that the choice be yours, when you came to know yourself fully."

She looked at him sharply and he bowed his head.

"I recall it," he said, and pressed his lips together before he uttered, "but . . ."

"You know that this village looks to my Lord Aeronymous; that we live within his honor and under his protection?"

He stared at her. Of course, he knew this; how could he not? Still, it seemed she waited for his answer, so he gave it, soft-voiced and patient as he might be.

"Yes, Mother, I know these things."

"Then have you taken thought—have you taken counsel of—this other power of yours, which is beyond us, and so much a part of you that you scarce understand it for power? Do you wish to place that power—whatever it is—in the service of my Lord Aeronymous, Cael Sojourner?"

"Mother—"

"Stay a moment and *think*! You might remain among us as always you have been—a guest, surrounded by our goodwill, giving to your host of yourself, as a good guest will, but . . . unremarked by my Lord; strange as they are, your powers would thus be protected by your solitary nature."

Such a solitary nature would mean that he could not share himself with . . . anyone.

Senaya.

Pain lanced through him, that they might not, that they never could complete their bonding. For what did he preserve himself, if his life thus became ashes and dust?

He raised his face to say this to the headwoman—and saw resignation in her face.

"I feared it would be thus. As the conscience and the protector of the village, I cannot but accept your gift freely given. My daughter has made her wishes plain; there is no one and nothing that might gainsay her. Certainly not her mother, who will be proud to welcome so able a son into her house—and a man of power into her village."

She extended her hands, palms up.

Cael placed his palms against hers, and felt his power rise. He gasped when a tithe of it left him, to bond with the headwoman's power . . .

And gasped again as her power flowed back, accepting; and tying him to the village.

"It is done," she said, then, lifting her hands away. "Go and be happy, Cael of Seafort."

• • • •

HAPPY HE WAS, AND FORTUNATE, too. He and Senaya brought their houses together as they had planned, and all the village joined to sing them into harmony.

As for the bond he shared with Senaya—he could not imagine life without that deep and certain source of love and strength. He wondered that he could have stood solitaire for so long. Surely, had he known the fullness of what he would share with Senaya, his pride would have melted before the knowledge.

Senaya, of course, served the village as healer and herbalist, just as before. He, having forsworn dangerous employment that took him beyond the ken of Seafort Village, cast about him for a needed service that met his skills.

He was able, and trained by his foster mother, thus he took up the jacket and the duties of a ranger. The forest of younger trees close to the village was generally safe enough, though willie wisps and other vermin would sometime venture near. Stranger things tended to arise beneath the elder trees, though, and it was the duty of the rangers to scout those territories and turn the strangest aside, far before they should endanger peaceful Seafort.

Indeed, he was precisely at the margin between the tame forest, hard by, but not within, the feral shadow of the elder trees, one fine mid-day. There had been market-day rumors regarding a child of the elder trees that perhaps had become over-bold, and approached the roads and outlying farmsteads too nearly.

He might have discounted such tales as boredom-bred, but the dogs of the village confided to him certain exotic scents, and unlikely sounds heard inside the night, at dawn-time, and sunset.

Those reports, he took seriously; much more so than the whispered tales of a shadow glimpsed by a farm-hedge, or the print of an unnatural foot in the clay by the edge of the river.

That morning, he had found the scent the dogs had given him at the village ward-stones, when he had crossed into the forest. It was fresh, and he followed, thinking to catch his quarry well before they came to the elder trees.

But the quarry's wood-lore was superior to his own; it gained the safety of its parent trees before Cael caught more than one troubling glimpse of it. Whereupon, he stood at the edge of the old forest, home of dangerous trees who held no love for his kind, and wondered whether he ought to follow . . . within.

The matter would need to be dealt with. Senaya gathered here, as did others, though most were wary of the old trees. Senaya, though—she feared nothing, and had told him, when he asked, that certain herbs gathered from beneath the shadow of the elder trees had more virtue than those found in the tamer part of the forest.

Still, the question remained before him—was today the day that Cael alone would enter the dark and silent wood, in pursuit of the trees' child? Or ought he return tomorrow, with a brace of his fellow rangers in support?

The scent was strong, feeding his hesitation. It was as if his quarry tarried in the shadows, watching him.

Taunting him? he wondered. Judging? There was no taint of fear upon the air, and that . . . was troubling.

Cautiously, curiously, he moved along the edge of the trees, just beyond the shadows' cold touch, and he came by that way to a small dug-out place, half-concealed by vegetation, and a small tumble of stone. He paused, for wolves often went to earth in such places to give birth.

Testing the air, he scented rock, and green things, and dust. If the place had once been a den, it was a den no longer.

He approached, and knelt at the opening to look within. The small space was empty, save for brittle bones, long gnawed clean and sifted over with silver sand. He sat back on his heels, then, looking up into the canopy, seeing how close the shadow of the elder trees fell, to this spot; this abandoned wolf's den.

"I found you alone, in the den, with bones about, and no need upon you," he recalled his foster mother's tale of his discovery. "You made no protest when I lifted you up and wrapped you in my sash to bear away."

His throat closed; it was hard to breathe; impossible to scent. Here? She had found him *here*, so near the elder wood that the shadow might well have fallen across the entry-way? And she had never told him?

But wait.

He felt Senaya's cool common sense rise in his blood, banishing panic. He had breath again, and the breeze brought him the information that the one he pursued had retreated further beneath the trees.

His foster mother had not shown him the spot where he had been found, though she had showed him much else among the tame trees. There were, after all, countless wolf-dens and fox-holes in the forest. To think that he had today stumbled upon the one where he—and so close—No.

No.

He was unsettled by the chase, disturbed by the strangeness of the quarry. So, there was one thing decided. He would pursue no further, alone, but return tomorrow, with comrades.

Having taken his decision, he rose, and walked a little further along the shadows' edge, all his senses on alert, seeking anything . . . else that might be amiss.

Satisfied at last that there was no other mischief lurking at the edge of the elder trees, and that the one he had followed here had, indeed, gone away, he turned back, toward the tame wood, and Seafort Village.

• • • •

HE HAD TOLD SENAYA about the den, and the wherefore of his fear. She would have felt his distress though their bond, but he wished her to know the process of his thought, especially in light of her mother's assertion that he held some power other than that which they all shared, and used, and—sometimes—plundered.

She heard him out, his Senaya, as they sat together on the bench in their garden, with the evening stealing up, the air cool and damp and tasting of the sea. When he had said all that was in his mind, she put him some few questions, then, setting her arms around him, drew his head down to her breast.

They rested thus while dusk grew into darkness. He was content enough to lie where she had put him; he might, indeed, have fallen quite asleep, save that he felt her thinking, through their bond, and it made him uneasy, that she need think so long, and so hard, upon the matter.

"Cael," she said, at last, and he felt her lips brush his forehead. "You know that you are my heart and that I love you beyond all else."

These were words that ought to have warmed; instead, they chilled him, and he would have sat up, so that he could look into her face, but her arms tightened, and he lay obedient, opening himself as much as possible to her through their bond; his nose bringing him the scent of her determination.

"I know that you love more than I love myself," he murmured. He felt a shiver along their bond; a flash of brilliant heat—and then he did sit up, breaking her grip without effort, and catching her hands in his when she would have embraced him again.

"Cael?"

"Your power rises," he said, looking down into her face. The glow suffused her, illuminating her from within, so that her face became like a moon, indeed, and brightened their little garden.

"Do you fear me?" she asked.

"No," he said, tasting truth on the back of his tongue.

"What do you think that I plan to do?" came the next question, and to that he could only shake his head. What could his Senaya *not* do, once her will was roused? He could only marvel upon her, and love her the more.

"You are beyond me," he told her, and kissed her glowing cheek, feeling her skin warm against his lips.

"Not that," she said. "Never that, my heart. I raise my power in order to properly ask a boon."

"A boon? We are one, Senaya; there is no need for asking between us!"

"In this thing, there is."

He felt her fingers flex against his palms, as she raised her face to meet his eyes.

"I would ask bride-right, my Cael."

For a moment, he was at a loss, and then he recalled it. Bride-right was more, and less, than the bond they now enjoyed, and it required permission. For what Senaya would do was capture his essence as he stood upon this hour and this day; and hold it within her own essence, as . . . a seed; a possible Cael who might be called into existence with the appropriate application of power. It was a thing not much used among the village-folk, who followed simple ways, but rather more used among the Great Ones, the lords and the ladies and the High Ozali, who had need to protect their power, and their holdings.

Cael drew a breath, and it was on his tongue-tip, the denial.

And then he bethought himself again.

Senaya wished to carry his essence, with its strange power, within herself, cuddled against her very soul.

It was, he realized, understanding her purpose in a flash, it was the most potent way available to her; to prove to him that she believed him no monster, or unnatural thing born from the spite of the elder trees.

And he—how could he doubt himself, when she carried him in her soul? It was a very great gift Senaya proposed to give to him—to them. All of their undertakings would be stronger, because of it.

He smiled at her then, and bent, only a little, to tenderly kiss her mouth. Then, he relinquished her hands and straightened his back.

Looking into her eyes, he smiled again.

"Yes," he said, and felt her power rise over him, and break, like a mighty wave against a stone.

• • • •

IT TOOK THE THREE SEAFORT rangers and three from Stonehold to track and trap the child of the elder trees, which had been fearsome, indeed. Both headwomen and three healers were required to unmake it.

When the thing was done, the folk of both villages came together for feasting, and merry-making, and the sharing about of power.

After the vanquishing of fear, and the celebration of victory, the affairs of both villages, and all the folk of them, slipped back into routine.

Of Senaya the Healer and Cael the Ranger, it was said that their bond grew stronger with every sunrise. Certainly, Cael found it so; Senaya's love was the constant star around which his life revolved; he was content; at peace in a way he had not thought possible. The village was all the world he wanted or needed; he felt himself perfectly fixed, and aptly rooted for the whole of his life.

And so he might have remained, had his duty taken him into the woods, rather than across the pastureland. He was to meet a husbandman there, and assist with mending a warding that his animals had grown too wise to heed. It was a fine day, with the taste of the ocean on the breeze. He strode on, light-footed with joy, when, piercing even the jubilation of the merrybells, came the call of a horn, closely followed by the belling of hounds.

Frowning, he paused, his hand against the trunk of a tree, listening until the horn sounded again.

No bone-made hunting horn, that. The tone was too high, with a hard edge that was only lent by metal. He had heard its like before, but only once. On that occasion, he had yet been serving as his foster mother's apprentice. She had drawn him away from the sound and the hunt, and when he had asked her why, she had looked on him, grim-eyed, and said that it was a horning—the lord's business and none of theirs.

He was his own man now, and had long ago learnt that the great lords in their power and their arrogance did sometimes hold those who displeased them in some manner until there was a house party or other gathering of their allies and peers. Then would the unfortunate prisoner be brought forth and a working performed to give them the seeming of a hart, or a fox, or some other prey.

In that form they would be hunted.

And in that form they would die.

He took a breath, recalling his foster mother's wisdom, for surely such a matter was beyond him, as were all the doings of the great.

Again the horn sounded, and the hounds shouted, much nearer now. He hesitated, listening with sharp ears, trying to gauge the progress of the hunt, and whether he ought turn aside.

Another breath, the breeze against his face, bringing him the tang of the ocean—and another scent, that set his hackles up.

For it was man he scented—laboring and afraid. That could only be the prey, and what the great lord Aeronymous was about to set his good hunting hounds upon a *man*, Cael had no notion.

But he intended to stop it.

He was already running, the scent full in his nose; the belling of hounds in his ears. His chosen course would intersect the path of the man and the dogs. If the quarry kept the pace, and Cael did not twist a leg in a gopher hole, then all could be managed: he would buy the prey time, though he doubted much profit would come of it; and he would prevent the dogs from tasting man-flesh.

Ahead of him, a white hart flashed from behind a small stand of trees. Cael threw himself forward, the breeze bringing him the unmistakable scent of man. He spun, digging the heels of his boots into the ground, facing back the way the hart had run.

Already, he could see the lead dogs, legs extended over the ground as if they were flying. They ran silent, now, which meant they had sighted their quarry. Cael settled himself more firmly onto the ground, and opened his arms.

It occurred to him, very distantly, that he was mad, to set himself between a hunting pack and its prey. These were no easy-going and garrulous village dogs such as he had known all his life. These—these were trained predators. Best outcome, they would flow around him, and shortly bring down the prey.

Worst, he would be mauled—or killed.

Despite the distant realization of his madness, he was not afraid. He was confident and at peace. They would neither harm him nor discount him, those swift-approaching beasts, with their long legs and their razor teeth. They would heed him; and he would keep them safe.

The pack leader was upon him, leaping from a distance, growl drowning the shriek of the merrybells. He caught the beast by the front legs and held him, looking deep into brown eyes, catching and holding the intelligence there.

There came the sense of contact, much as with the village dogs; the leader asserting his superiority—and Cael asserting his own. Slowly, Cael impressed his will; impressed calmness; impressed sense, for this noble fellow—this Scartooth—he was no man-killer, but an honest dog, a strong leader, and a mighty hunter. Cael approved of Scartooth, and Scartooth approved of Cael. Scartooth was happy to be with Cael.

Scartooth, indeed, would do all and anything that Cael asked, for Cael was leader, and Scartooth so acknowledged him.

. . . by the time the horses and the lords arrived, the pack was lolling on the meadow-grass at his feet, and Cael was softly caressing Scartooth's ragged ears.

• • • •

THE GREAT ONES BURNED so brightly that Cael wished to close his eyes; the weight of their power like to crush him to his knees.

However, he neither averted his eyes, nor knelt before their radiance. It was his to protect the pack; and so he stood tall and met the sea-blue eyes of the forward rider.

"Well, here's a twist," said the other great one, who sat a stone-grey horse like a boulder come to life. "What's to do, Aeronymous?"

"Why, now we test our skill at tracking," blue-eyed Aeronymous said, his voice light and even, as if finding his hunters taking their ease in the middle of a hunt was entirely unsurprising, even expected.

"You, boy! Take the pack to their kennel, and tend them till I call!"

Power struck him, hard, augmenting the light command; he felt the need to obey, precisely, sink into his bones, and become his own will.

He bowed to the honor of Lord Aeronymous.

Straightening, he patted Scartooth on the shoulder.

"Home," he murmured.

The dog moved forward, Cael at his side, and the others leapt to their feet to follow.

The horses and the lords swept around them, on the trail of the one who wore the seeming of a white hart. Last to pass him was one who smelled of the pack. Scartooth favored him with a glance, before nipping a youngling who lay still in the meadow grass.

"What have you done?" whispered the man—the dog-master, he must be, Cael realized.

"Prevented the dogs from learning that man is prey," he answered, more sharply than he had intended.

The dog-master's face paled. He licked his lips, then kicked his horse and rode away through the silver dust raised by the lords' horses.

Cael shrugged, and said again to Scartooth, "Home."

• • • •

THERE HAD BEEN NO COMPULSION that they hurry, only that they return. Thus they went leisurely, hunting on the move. The dogs knew their business, and by the time they passed through the small gate, there were three rabbits and a brace of forest-hens in Cael's game sack.

They crossed the green, Cael at the head of the pack, and Scartooth at his side, his ragged ears held high, and his head at the level of Cael's belt. The compulsion was stronger now, to find the kennel quickly, but not so strong that he was unable to stop when an arms-man approached, and said, quietly, "Stay."

There was a little power in that command, but nothing to override the lord's geas.

Cael stopped of his own will and looked into the man's eyes.

"Who are you?" the arms-man asked.

"Cael of Seafort," he answered. "Lord Aeronymous sends me to kennel the hounds, and to bide with them till he calls."

The arms-man nodded slowly, and made as if to step back.

"Hold," Cael said, and offered the game sack. "For the kitchen, if you would. I do not think I can deviate so much."

Indeed, it would seem that he had already remained in one spot too long; his feet were shifting against the grass.

"I'll take it," the arms-man said. "Go—the lord is not gentle with those who try him."

"My thanks," Cael said, and the pack moved on through the gate in good order, and the young ones running for the water, while Cael kept walking to the very center of the place, whereupon the will of Aeronymous released him, and he heard the gate snap shut at his back.

· · · ·

HE LAY AGAINST SCARTOOTH'S back, the rest of the pack lying as close as possible, their joy in his presence warming him as much as the heat from their bodies. The dogs, simple and honest as they were, slept. He, less simple and perhaps not so honest as he had always supposed himself, lay awake, staring up at the stars like jewels in the night sky.

The bond he shared with Senaya seemed . . . less strong in this place that was laced with so much power, and so many workings that his skin itched, and his eyes burned. He did his best to tend it, the bond; Senaya might not know where he was, nor how long he might be away, but he was determined that she not be in fear for his life.

Lord Aeronymous—well, there had been a warning, had there not, from the arms-man? Lord Aeronymous was not gentle with those who thwarted him. He must, therefore, expect to be punished. He did not think that the lord would unmake him;

it seemed to him that his impertinence in interrupting the lord's pleasure was not worth that. There had, however, been the other lord, before whom Aeronymous had been disadvantaged . . .

No, it was impossible to guess what Lord Aeronymous might do, he decided, and his thoughts turned again to his determination to stop the hunt, and to preserve the integrity of the dogs.

Since childhood, he had easy discourse with the village dogs; they deferred to him, and mentioned odd smells and movements to him. That was merely . . . who he was. He did understand that others did not enjoy the same level of intimacy with the dogs—even Senaya did not. But, then, Senaya's gift was healing; she had no need to speak with dogs.

That he had dared place himself between a pack and its prey—that amazed him yet, and, at the same time, it surprised him not at all, that the dogs had come to him, and placed their wills in service to his. He had expended no power; he had merely . . . stretched himself beyond the familiar mold of husband and ranger, as if he had straightened to his full height after years of standing stooped.

He heard footsteps, coming toward the kennel, and a subtle chime, as if metal struck metal. Around him, the dogs lifted their heads, noses up, testing the air. He did the same, scenting power, and beneath it, the scent of the arms-man who had relieved him of the game-bag.

Cael stood, and Scartooth stood, also. He placed his hand on the hound's shoulder, and murmured to the rest of them, "Stay. Friends."

"Cael of Seafort," came the voice of Aeronymous. "Come forth alone to make an account of your actions to your liege lord."

He felt the power snatch at him, jerking him forward like a doll. Apparently, Lord Aeronymous did not care to give a man the choice of obeying from his own heart.

Pulled by power, he came to the kennel's door, and only then realized that Scartooth paced him yet.

"Stay," he murmured.

The hound whined, close in his throat, echoing the distress growing in Cael's breast. Whined once—and obeyed.

On the green, Lord Aeronymous stood at the center of a nimbus of light, his green curls all tumbled 'round his shoulders, as if he were come fresh from his bed.

"Stand," he said, his voice as cold as ocean spray, and Cael stopped where he was. He heard the arms-man move, and the sound of the kennel's gate being firmly shut.

"So, Cael of Seafort, why have you not come to my attention ere this?" asked Aeronymous.

"My lord, there was no need, that you notice one ranger more than another."

"But such an *unusual* ranger," Aeronymous murmured, and then snapped, "What did you do to my hounds, sirrah?"

That was accompanied by a lash of power, burning as it broke across his cheek.

Cael took a breath.

"I prevented them from learning that man is prey. They are good dogs—hunting dogs. To use them to hunt men—it was a corruption of their service, my lord."

He braced himself for another blow, and was mildly surprised when it did not come.

"The criminal they chased was horned, exactly to prevent this lesson of man as prey from being learnt."

Cael shook his head.

"He smelled like a man yet, my lord. I caught the scent myself. The dogs knew what they hunted."

There was a long pause, in which power snapped and glittered, but none struck him.

Inside his halo of light, Aeronymous inclined his stately head.

"For the sake of my hounds, I thank you, Cael Dog-Friend. Come with me now."

With that, Aeronymous turned and marched off, a line of power sunk deep into Cael's chest, so that he was pulled along in the lord's wake, like a child's toy. The arms-man kept pace, and Cael smelled his dismay.

He scented them in the instant before the lord exerted his power, compelling Cael to leap down into a pit. Smelled them; heard them—and, landing with bent knees, saw them, as the lord threw his nimbus wide.

Wolves.

Coats brindled, and eyes red-shot, half-mad with their confinement. They growled, all three as one. Cael dropped to one knee, seeking the red gaze of the wolf before him. Teeth showed, the growl came to a crescendo; and Cael felt the connection made; breathed in, waiting...

The wolf threw himself onto his back, paws waving in the air. Cael leaned in to rub the lean belly, while the other two jostled him, licking his face and hands.

Kneeling, he opened his heart, and allowed their untamed nature to rise into him, stirring his blood, freshening his courage.

"Cael of Seafort, come to me!"

He felt the tug of the lord's will, augmenting the command. He resisted the compulsion, though doing so waked a pain like a dagger through his breast.

"My lord!" he called out. "I obey you, but in my time. There is delicate business afoot, and I cannot say what will happen, if I am suddenly removed from it."

There was a slight pause, in which he thought he heard the arms-man gasp. Then came the voice of Aeronymous once more.

"Do not by any means endanger yourself," he said. "You become precious to me, Cael the Wolf, and I would not see thee harmed. I leave here at your service Erdin, my arms-man sworn. He will lower a rope to you when you ask for it. You will—in your time, of course!—place yourself in his hands, for he has my orders concerning you."

"Yes," Cael whispered, drinking in what the wolves would give him: stealth, cunning, loyalty, fierce devotion.

Wolf ears heard the lord's departure; wolf senses noted the man left behind, shivering in the cold sea air. Cael and the wolves dreamed red dreams and gold together, until they faded.

The wolves slept. Cael rose, stiff with long kneeling, walked to the edge of the pit and called quietly for Erdin to lower the rope.

• • • •

DAWN WAS PAINTING BRONZE streaks across the velvet sky when he was ushered—fed, bathed, and dressed in tunic and leggings provided by the House—into the presence of his lord. Into, as Erdin whispered to him before he knocked upon the door, my lord's private chambers.

Erdin misliked this private meeting, though Cael was at a loss to know why. He might have asked the arms-man, but the door swung open then, and they entered a room done 'round in shelves, each groaning beneath a weight of books. Aeronymous sat in a white conch by the window, a book open, but unregarded upon his lap. His head was turned, the green curls orderly now; and it appeared that he watched the progress of the dawn.

"My lord," said Erdin, "the ranger Cael is here."

"In his own time," my lord murmured, without turning his head. "Leave him; and find yourself some rest."

Erdin hesitated, and it seemed to Cael that he would speak, save Aeronymous, his face turned toward the window, tipped his head just slightly, as if listening closely for some particular sound.

The arms-man swallowed and bowed.

"Yes, my lord," he said, and shot a sharp glance at Cael before he strode away into the hallway.

The door closed behind him.

Slowly, then, the shell-chair turned, until Aeronymous was fully facing the room. Cael met the sea-blue eyes, then, recalling himself, bowed to the lord's honor.

When he straightened, he met the lord's eyes again, and waited.

"You are bold," Aeronymous said musingly. "Perhaps Erdin failed of telling you that I find boldness . . . impertinent."

"He did say so, sir," Cael admitted, not wishing to cause the arms-man harm.

"But you chose to ignore him. Or you do not think it impertinent that a ranger boldly meet the eyes of a lord."

There seemed nothing to say to this that might not be construed as continuing impertinence—Erdin had warned him, also, that Aeronymous counted slights with a heavy hand.

"Well," Aeronymous said, closing his book. It rose from his knee, and wafted to the shelf on the right of the chair, where it inserted itself into the space from which it must have been summoned.

Cael kept his eyes turned toward the lord, his gaze somewhat averted, so that he did not give challenge by a direct stare.

"Well," Aeronymous said again. "You have convinced me, Cael the Wolf, that you must become attached to my household."

Cael drew a breath. "I had no wish to do so, my lord," he said, softly, his gaze averted.

"Of that, I am certain," Aeronymous said. "Indeed, I had thought to let you go with a beating, and a tithe of your power given in liege-gift. But there is no help for either of us; you must become mine."

Panic rose in him; he quelled it, and bowed, as courtly as he was able.

"My lord, I have a place, and there I serve you well. I –"

Aeronymous waved a hand. "Yes, yes," he said impatiently. "You have a bond-mate, and a life, and your duty, wherein you served me, *in your way*, I make no doubt." The blue eyes had taken on grey, as if storm clouds moved over the ocean. "You ought to have thought of these things before you turned my dogs from their task, and brought yourself to my attention. You ought, perhaps, to have allowed the wolves to kill you. But you did not the one, and failed of the other, and thus the case falls to me."

He stood, then, power outlining his form, and his curls stirring, as if in a sea-breeze.

"You are too dangerous a man, Cael the Wolf, to be left to your own will and judgment. You would ever be a blade at my back. If blade you would be, then you will be safely sheathed, and hung upon *my* belt."

"My lord, I mean you no harm. I –"

"Silence!"

A blow struck his chin, snapping his mouth shut. Within that sealed cavern, his tongue began to burn.

He reached, blindly, to his own poor store of power, bringing it, icy, into his mouth. Surprisingly, the lord allowed it; he allowed the fire to be quenched. But he did not allow Cael to unseal his lips.

"Hear me, now, for there is a choice to be made—one of the few that remain to you. Either you will release your bond of your own will, or I will break it, of mine. Understand that some damage might be done, if I am the author of this action, and I think you will agree that it would be a sad pity, were Seafort deprived of its healer. Choose carefully, Cael the Wolf."

His blood was hot with his risen power; he was terrified for Senaya—and as before, there was neither thought nor uncertainty, as he straightened into that other power, which was his alone—and called.

From the kennels, came the belling of hounds. From further yet, came the howling of wolves.

He felt himself expand further still, and in some interior room a lap-dog began to yip. He would free himself; he would be not be bound here; he—

A blade of power slashed through him, and he screamed, his lips tearing open, before he fell, insensible, to the foam-colored rug.

· · · ·

"WAKE!"

He tasted blood as he straightened his back—and felt the bite of restraints, around arms and legs; his throat was gripped, tight and cold, and when he moved his head to worry at it, he heard the clank of chain.

At last he opened his eyes, saw one end of the chain in the hand of Aeronymous, and felt the metal biting into his skin.

"Are you a fool, Cael the Wolf? Speak!"

"No, my lord," he heard himself say, though he had willed no answer.

"I take leave to doubt it. Did you think to best me? Did you think to break away? Rousing my own dogs against me, in the depths of my own holding? Would you slay your lord? Put your paltry, peasant happiness before the command of your liege? However you came to be, your only purpose is to *obey me*. You live at my whim, and when you have served me to the fullness of your meager ability, I will drink you down in one quaff, Cael the Wolf. Do these things please you? Speak!"

"Yes, master," he heard himself say, and hated the words.

"You have now demonstrated to both of us why it is that you must on no account be allowed your own will. Perhaps it was necessary. Allow me now to recall to you your penultimate choice. Do you break the bond, or do I break the healer? You have shown me no reason to be gentle."

Senaya. No, he would not give Senaya to the lord's cruelty. But . . . to break faith with her whom he shared . . . everything? Such a sundering must unmake one—or both!—as close as their sharing had been.

He took a breath, and looked to his lord.

"Speak," said Aeronymous.

"I will do it," he said, his voice hoarse.

"Then be about it, quickly!"

He closed his eyes, and found the bond lying hard against his heart, quivering with Senaya's distress. Her mother was with her, and the eldest of her sisters. Good. They would do what was needful, and keep her away from harm.

The proper way to break a bond, is to cut it in the middle, so that neither side suffers more from the severing than is . . . needful.

Cael brought his will and his intent to his own heart, concentrating on the bond until it filled his entire awareness.

He brought the knife of his will down, severing the bond with a single strike.

And screamed again, as power poured out of him like blood, and his heart shattered in his breast. Blackness overtook him; he embraced it. Somewhere, he heard a dog howling, and in the woods, deep in the woods, shrouded in emerald light, he saw something move four-footed among the fallen leaves, and rise up on two legs to face the wolf . . .

. . . wolf . . .

It was cold. The wolf faded, and the wood. He reached out to touch Senaya—and found . . . nothing.

• • • •

FIRE FELL OUT OF COLD nothingness, assaulting his last fluttering thought. Power poured into him, scalding; scouring. His mouth was filled with salt, and his ears with the crashing of waves. His sundered heart was fire-forged; melted and made whole; the howl that he heard was his own, until—at last and again—he heard nothing at all.

• • • •

HE CAME TO HIMSELF. His cheek was pressed to the rug; the bonds and the collar were gone. There was a . . . weight at the center of his chest, but there was no pain.

There was no pain.

"You may rise and look upon your liege lord, Cael the Wolf."

The voice thrilled him; he rose eager, and raised his eyes, gasping in an agony of love. He dropped to his knees, tears springing to his eyes, but he was not ashamed, for was this not his liege-lord, whom he loved above all else?

"Are you in truth my faithful wolf?"

"Yes, my lord."

"It pleases me to hear it. Raise your face to me—yes. Do you love me, Cael?"

"Only you, my lord."

Aeronymous stepped forward and held out his slim hand.

"Swear to me, if that is your will."

Of course it was his will! He placed his hand into the hand of his lord, and gazed up into those sea-blue eyes.

"I, Cael, do swear upon my soul that I will keep faith with Aeronymous and never cause him harm. I will defend him and reverence him and in all things obey him; and stand his man forevermore."

There was a faint boom, as if a door had shut, and a sharp pain at the center of his chest—gone before he could gasp. He felt a glow of happiness.

"Excellent," his lord said. "We shall never part, Cael the Wolf. Your oath binds you to Aeronymous, for lack of whom you will die. Does that please you?"

Something stirred at the back of his mind, showing teeth in a silent snarl, but that was as nothing before the joy that suffused him.

"I am pleased, my liege."

A smile came onto those cold lips.

"Hear me, then. You will serve me as Master of Hounds. The first task you are given is to become court-wise and handy, for my Master of Hounds will sit at the second highest table, and be the equal of those who style themselves noble. You will be my eyes and my ears, and you will report all that you have heard, to me, and me alone."

Behind him, he heard the door open, but he remained on his knees, looking up into his lord's face. He could have remained so for the rest of his life, and wanted for nothing else.

However, his lord had other necessities.

"Rise," Aeronymous said, and he did so, anticipating the opportunity to serve.

Aeronymous gestured, and one came forward, splendid in courtly dress, scented with book dust; his power heavy with knowledge.

"You will go with this one," his lord said, "and learn all that is taught to you."

"Yes, my lord." He bowed; straightened, and hesitated.

"Speak," said Aeronymous.

"Yes, my lord. I only wonder . . . Will I *see* you?"

Once again Aeronymous was seen to smile.

"I will be with you always, my wolf, for are we not of one heart?"

• • • •

HE WAS AN EXEMPLARY wolf—intelligent, loyal, and fierce. In those early days, he mastered every lesson set to him, quickly and thoroughly. History, custom, court courtesy and dialect, the deportment expected of one who sat among lords—those things he learned easily. Arms work and hand-to-hand—those he barely needed to learn; it was if he had been born with an innate understanding of such matters. Horsemanship, however, had been a long road, for horses did not like him. Even now he rode but rarely, though he had long since mastered the spell-work to force his mount to calm obedience.

Having been schooled in the basics, he was placed as his lord had said—at the second table, among those who were great, but who had ambition. He listened, as he had been directed, and he repeated what his keen ears heard, to no one but Aeronymous. Indeed, his happiest moments were those spent sitting at his lord's feet in the private parlor, reporting and then listening as Aeronymous told over what this or that nugget might mean; who must be culled, and who left to continue until it was seen what others joined with him, in an attempt to bring Aeronymous down from his high seat, drink his power, and set themselves up as Sea Ozali in his stead.

He had brought the tales of such plots to his lord, as he was bound to do; and he stood by his lord's side, when punishment was extracted. That, too, was something to learn, but Aeronymous did not always—or even often—mete death to those who would have gladly served him that dish.

Of one, he drew power, rendering his enemy invalid and scarce able to defend himself. It would have been kinder merely to kill him; but his lord Aeronymous was not kind.

It was *more effective* to return him, trembling and frail, to the ranks of his sometime allies. To them he spoke, for the few days longer that he managed to survive; he told them of the cold will of Aeronymous, and his power that was too great to be taken. So, he taught them, if neither fear nor respect, at least caution.

Of another plotter, he merely drew the names of her compatriots, and let her return to her place, unscathed; undiminished in honor. Not so, those whose names had been taken; those, Aeronymous broke slowly, partaking of their power a sip at a time, savoring their suffering. He had required Cael by his side for this, and fed him also tit-bits of power; scraps from the feast table.

Still a third, he reached out to at a state dinner, and drew his power all at once, killing him where he sat; the thing so deftly done that none but Cael understood it had happened until the guests rose from the table, for dancing.

In this way, by these stratagems, did Aeronymous keep his seat and grow his power. He was an awful lord, but one who protected all within his care.

Save they did not try him.

For his part, Cael was content. The love he held for his lord was constant; it could not be otherwise. He knew that those other servants of Aeronymous feared him, but it mattered little. There were those who did not fear him, and who welcomed him with uncomplicated joy. He visited the dogs often, as this thing had not been denied him by his lord, and he reveled in their simple honesty.

He was, indeed, on his way to the kennels even now.

It was rare for him to be free at so early an hour in the evening, but Lord Aeronymous had lately acquired a new favorite, and it was his pleasure to retire them early for disport and enjoyment. This was the third favorite Cael had seen; and he wished she would eventually be cast from the lord's bedchamber as the first had been—pleased, somewhat increased in power, and hung about with trinkets.

The second . . . had not fared so well. He had presumed upon the lord's infatuation, mistaking indulgence for weakness.

Aeronymous was never weak. And it had been, Cael had reflected at the time, a terrible thing to have fallen from favorite to traitor, for the lord had been as full with his fury as he had been with his brighter passion.

Cael shivered as he made his way toward the kennel, and not only because the ocean air was chill. It was well, he thought, that Aeronymous had fixed his own regard and nature in the moment of his resurrection. Whatever he had lost in his love for the lord, at least he risked no death such as had been meted the second favorite.

He came 'round the corner of the house, following the path that skirted the kitchen garden—and froze, a step echoing in his ear.

There was no footstep among the House which was strange to him, but this—a soft footfall by nature, purposeful by intent; familiar, and beloved, long before he had come to the House of Aeronymous.

The breeze danced 'round the edge of the house, bringing him her scent, and he spun, horror replacing his content, searching the path with his keen, hound's eyes . . .

She stepped out from the kitchen doorway, and stood in the center of the path, her hands folded beneath her cloak, and her dark hair lying loose upon her shoulders.

"Senaya!" He could not move—but she did, walking slowly down the path to him, outlined by the meager glow of her power.

"So, you remember me. It was said in the village that Lord Aeronymous had rent your past from you."

He shook his head, trembling now, horror rooting him yet to the path.

"I remember," he said. "Senaya—"

"You glow like the moon, my Cael. Surely, you are a lord, yourself."

"No," he said harshly. "I am my lord's lapdog, with his collar 'round my heart."

It frightened him, that he spoke those words. He had known, of course; Aeronymous had *not* taken his memories, nor hidden the manner of his binding—that would have been kind. Still, he had been content to let the knowledge lie sleeping beneath what he had become.

"I see it," Senaya said, stopping now that they were toe to toe. "He has hurt you, my Cael, and grievously. You were not meant, ever, to be chained."

"It is too late, as you must see. Senaya—you must not bide here! He will—I do not know what he will do, but he threatened once to break you, and—"

"And you would not allow it. I know; I was there with you, through the bond, until the moment you broke us asunder. I thought then that I would die. My mother thought that, surely, you had." She paused, tipping her head, perhaps to study him more closely.

"My sister said that you *wished* to die."

"I had. I . . . did. My lord caught my soul before it took flight."

"And bound it to his service, twisting you as he did so."

"Senaya, this is of no use. I am lost to you, as if I had died, in truth. Go, I beg you—"

"You are afraid," she murmured. "For me. This is more than I had hoped for."

"Should I not be afraid for you? I love you!"

He gasped, pain searing him, as if someone had wrung his living heart in a vise.

"Cael?"

He shook his head, breathing against the agony until it grew bearable, hearing his blurted words again, tasting the simple truth of them. And that was worse—far worse than mere pain. If anyone had heard, who would bear the tale to Aeronymous; if the sea-breeze wafted those words to his lord's sharp ears . . .

"Senaya, you *must* go."

She smiled and lay her hand on his shoulder. "Why, and so I shall, very soon. I had only wished to see you again, my Cael; and to give you a gift."

A gift? He had no need of gifts; his one pressing need was to see her safe away. Already, he was planning; he might send Scartooth and Vinja with her, to guard her way back to the village. They were good dogs, and true; they would let nothing harm her.

"Peace, my love," she murmured. "Recall, when we were bonded, I asked bride-right, and you granted it?"

"Yes. . ." He remember the feel of her power enveloping him; how he had trembled at her strength . . .

"We are no longer bonded, and I wish to marry again. Thus, I return to you your nature."

"My nature." He dared to extend a hand, and touch her dear face. "Senaya, hear me. I am a child of the old wood; an unnatural thing. What you hold is . . . a monster. Cast it from you."

She turned her cheek into his caress. "No monster, but an honest man, and true, who even now plots to see me safely away, discounting any cost to himself." She took a breath, and moved one careful step back from him.

"Hear me, now, Cael who was bondmate to Senaya; this thing that our lord has imposed upon you—it is not love, no matter how great a burden it casts upon your heart. Allow it to rule you and you will become a monster, indeed. I return to you your nature, that you may have a true guide, untainted by our lord's power."

Her power flared, and broke, a minor wavelet, spending at his feet. There was no other sensation, save his sadness, that he should have so far outgrown her; who had only wished to be her equal. It struck him then, like a rock to the chest; power flared, igniting him, blood and bone. Senaya swam in his vision, and he heard a dog whine, near at hand.

His sight left him entirely as he went to his knees on the path; he felt Senaya's arms come 'round him tightly, and her lips seek his.

"No . . ." he managed, feeling his power hungrily yearn toward her. "Senaya . . ."

"Yes," she whispered. "I would marry again, my Cael; I would never again be without you."

His younger self, burning yet into his bones, ached for her, his power, gained from Aeronymous, hungered to consume her. He trembled, and sought to put her from him, but all she need do was press her lips to his ear and murmur two fateful words.

"Freely given."

She flowed into him, cool and wise and constant—so little, and so quickly absorbed by the hungry fires of his power.

He felt her diminish in his grasp, and held her closer, but she melted even as his arms tightened. Crying out, he wrenched his eyes open, and beheld her, translucent in the moonlight, the stars glowing through her, like jewels.

Then came a breeze, tasting of salt and seaweed . . . And she was gone.

Cael, called the Wolf, knelt on the path in the moonlight, his heart like a stone in his breast; and next to it, another stone, as light as the first was heavy.

And flowing through the currents of his power, cool and wise and strong, he felt her, and knew they would never again be parted.

The Road to Pomona's

¶ *Elinor.*" He sighed; she was off *again*. You'd think she didn't want—

"Hmm? Did you say something, Charles?"

"Did I say—Elinor, we are trying here to plan our vacation—something I think we *both* want very much?" It was lost on her. She only looked at him, face composed, eyes empty of any hint of emotion. Of involvement.

He tried a different tack, pushing the papers and travel brochures together into a hasty pile and stacking them atop the refrigerator, theoretically out of the cat's territory.

"Listen, I'm beat, myself. Tomorrow's Saturday, we'll have the whole day to just mess around and talk about plans. It was stupid to try it tonight, anyway. Let's go to—"

Amazement stopped him. Elinor was sitting stiffly upright, face, for once, intent. "What did you say?"

"What did I—when?" He was honestly baffled.

"You said tomorrow's Saturday. *Saturday*. It can't possibly be Saturday . . . "

"It can't?" Charles stared. "Why can't it? I've waited a whole—"

Again, her face interrupted him. "OK, suppose *you* tell *me* what day tomorrow is."

She looked a little bewildered herself. "Well, all right—Saturday. I guess. It's just that I promised Pomona—"

"Pomona? Who's Pomona? And why'd you promise her anything? You knew perfectly well that this is the first Saturday I've had off in—HEY!"

But Elinor was already gone, racing down the short hallway to their bedroom.

• • • •

THE ROAD TO POMONA'S is tree-lined and dim. You move for a timeless time over white gravel, the breeze that cools your face scented with roses and lilac. Suddenly, you stand out upon the hillside and there it is, set like a jewel in the very heart of the valley, an island of serenity in a sea of deep red grass ...

• • • •

"ELINOR? ELINOR, WHY'RE you sitting in the dark?"

She stirred, focused. "I've got a headache. The light bothers me."

"Oh." He moved into the room, sat on the corner of the bed. She could just see him, a dim, slumped-forward outline, hands clenched between his knees.

"Listen, Elinor . . . ." He paused.

"I'm listening, Charles."

"I—well, *look*, if you don't want the vacation, or you want to go someplace else—I mean, you should *say* so, right? It's not like we have to—I just thought—hell, all the overtime I've been doing, we ought to get something out of it. But if you'd rather not . . . "

"Oh, no. No, Charles, Las Vegas sounds *lovely*—" she suppressed the mental image of hot, bright lights; too many bodies; too much noise. "I think we'll have *lots* of fun. Really I do."

The outline of his shoulders straightened in the dimness. "That's the truth, now?"

"Cross my heart." She moved to sit beside him; rested her forehead against his arm. "I warned you, didn't I? I'm impossible. I *told* you so—moody, irascible. But, no, nothing would do but that you marry the wench—" She pounded him lightly on the back with one half-serious fist. "I *warned* you, you bully—"

He laughed; swung an arm around to pull her close. "OK, you did. The blame's on me. Sometimes, it's almost worth it ..."

Much later, at the very edge of dreaming, he remembered.

"Elinor. Who's Pomona?"

He was already asleep when she answered, "Oh, nobody—really."

She woke before him next morning; snuck away for a quick shower; pulled on jeans and a bright red sweater and went down the hall to the kitchen, running fingers through still-damp hair.

The cat was fed first, as always, she murmuring breakfast pleasantries; he aloof, but polite. She clicked on the radio, pushed open the window above the sink and turned back, hands on hips, to frown around the kitchen. "Pancakes, I think?" and then grinned. "Why not? Saturday comes but once a week—"

Eggs, milk, and sausage were out of refrigerator like a conjuring trick; the skillet was set to heat and the coffeepot primed. She sang with the radio as she worked. The breeze came through the window, carrying the scent of fresh-mown grass from the park across the street.

• • • •

THE ROAD TO POMONA'S *is tree-lined and dim. You move for a timeless time over white gravel, the breeze that cools your face scented with roses and lilac. Suddenly, you stand out upon the hillside and there it is, set like a jewel in the very heart of the valley; an island of serenity in a sea of deep red grass. And within, Pomona herself, whose house is but a reflection of her own deep and healing peace. She busies herself, perhaps, at her spinning, or makes music upon a crystalline*

keyboard. Though, again, perhaps not today. For tonight there is to be
celebration in Pomona's house, and there are preparations to be made.
Best you not tarry, then, upon the hill; for here is one place where
actuality surpasses anticipation.

"Morning, Spike!" She felt herself whirled about, mechanically
returned an exuberant kiss. "Pancakes, huh? Super! *Real* coffee?
Time for a fast shower? I'll be right back—save some for me, now!"

She was humming with the radio again by the time he returned.

They ate, Charles putting pancakes into his mouth at an
alarming rate and, at the same time, chattering about the proposed
trip to Vegas. Elinor pushed bits of soggy pancake and sausage
around her plate, remembering to glance up every now and then,
and smile.

He ran down, finally, and leaned back in his chair, third cup of
coffee held reverently in his hands, and grinned at her. "My dear,
you have outdone yourself. If this is what I miss by working on
Saturday—"

The road to Pomona's is tree-lined and dim—

She was jerked to her feet, "—to the zoo!" Charles was
laughing.

"The zoo?" The shock of transition made her stupid.

"Sure, the zoo. It's bright sunshine; we should take advantage."
He leaned forward conspiratorially, "I'll buy you an ice cream."
Then he was charging to the front door, Elinor in tow.

"The dishes!" she cried.

"Let the cat do 'em!"

And they raced down the apartment-house stairs and into the
street, laughing identical laughter.

• • • •

THE ROAD TO POMONA'S is tree-lined and dim. You walk for a timeless time over white gravel, the breeze that cools your face scented with roses and lilac. Suddenly, you stand out upon the hillside and there it is, set like a jewel in the very heart of the valley; an island of serenity in a sea of deep red grass. Dusk is approaching now and already candles are being lit in the windows to show the way to those few who do not know it by heart. A festival tonight, the candlelight murmurs across the valley; a celebration for our true friend, our Elinor. Come, come all, to meet Elinor; to welcome Elinor . . .

". . . Elinor. Come to bed." He sat next to her on the loveseat, reached out uncertainly. "Hey, are you all right? I mean, can I get you anything or something?" His hand smoothed her short, rough hair. "Spike? You there?"

She focused slowly, read the concern in his face, made the effort: "Too much excitement today, I guess. I'm not used to doing much on Saturdays, since you've been working. I'm a little—keyed up."

He looked relieved. "Keyed up, eh? Well, ol' Doc Charles has a cure for *that*, little lady. Just you stay right here one minute while I mix it up."

He vanished, and she heard him rummaging in the kitchen. His minute stretched into five while she carefully noted the signs of wear in the carpet; the pattern of the traffic light on the shade.

It *had* to be tonight—the Gate would only admit her fully tonight. Elinor closed her eyes, hearing Pomona's voice explaining it, over the *sshussh* of her spinning: "It will not be difficult. You already know the way . . . To the ones you leave on the other side—it will only look to them as if you had died."

Charles thrust a warm mug into her hand. "Down the hatch."

She swallowed obediently. Warm milk and brandy.

"All of it."

She showed him the empty mug. He took it back to the kitchen, reappeared and pulled her to her feet.

"Now to bed." A finger across her lips stifled a fledgling protest. "Don't argue with your doctor, girl; he knows best. Woman your age needs her sleep. So, c'mon; let's tuck you in."

After he had turned off the light and settled in his side of the bed, she murmured, "Charles?"

"Hmm?"

"I love you, Charles."

"I love you, too, Spike. G'night."

"Good-bye."

• • • •

THE ROAD TO POMONA'S...

The Vestals of Midnight

You've been there, right? The moment when you're startled out of a sound sleep because someone is walking on your land who doesn't belong there?

Who *seriously* doesn't belong there?

Curled on my side, eyes closed, snugged into blankets still warm from Borgan's presence, I reached for the Land . . .

It was early—or late, depending on your inclination and service. Borgan'd left ten minutes ago, to go out for the day's fishing. Those who prospered in the dark were thinking about pulling themselves into their places for a snooze, while those who had no cause to hide from the sun's face were drifting toward wakefulness. . .

There.

I snatched at the shiver of wrongness; pushed the Land to *show me*; and sat up straight in bed.

There?

Who in God's name would try to sneak up on the Enterprise?

I mean, the Enterprise *is* on my Land – by which I mean, it's in Archers Beach, of which I am, for a bunch of complicated reasons, mostly having to do with sin, and bloodlines, and—I'm sorry—magic, the Guardian. Geography being what it is, the Enterprise is in my—call it *my jurisdiction*. In theory, this means it's also under my authority.

Feel free to tell that to the Enterprise. I'll wait.

Still keeping a tight fix on that sliver of wrongness on the Land, I opened my mundane eyes to my bedroom. Breccia the cat was sitting up tall at the bottom of the bed, ridiculous floof of a tail wrapped primly around her toes; her eyes serious. Outside, I could hear the ocean playing with the shore; the view out the window was grey sea-mist against dawn-grey sky.

The imminent rising of the sun was causing the stranger on my Land some concern, and they weren't making any particular effort to hide that worry—or themselves.

Which in turn worried *me*.

I threw back the covers, pulled on jeans, sweater, socks, sneakers; nodded to Breccia.

"Hold the fort," I told her. "Be right back."

Then I reached to the Land again, and stepped from my bedroom . . .

Into the dooryard of the Enterprise, which was shrouded in something much denser and more malevolent than mere fog; heavy with a despair that reminded me forcibly of a Black Dog.

There was magic building. Specific, sophisticated, magic, and the Enterprise was its intended target. I drew on my own power, and looked closer, seeing the sticky ball of compulsion and command revolving in the thick air; saw, more importantly, the dark figure at the heart of the darkness, cloak billowing in a breeze I didn't feel; the spell very nearly complete, spinning between the palms of their hands, spitting sticky black sparks of malice.

I took a deep breath, drew a tad more power, and spoke.

"That," I said, conversationally, "would be a bad mistake."

The Land boomed; the air crackled. The dark figure jumped, the bomb they'd created snapping out of existence with a pettish little *fsst*, like a wet firecracker.

A breeze rushed through the clearing, chilly and tasting of salt. The unnatural fog shredded, and I was facing a stocky woman wearing a long black gown under the black cloak, bodice laced with blood-red ribbons, sleeves dripping with crimson lace. Her face was pale and round, and she was wearing sunglasses.

"How dare you interfere with me?" she snapped.

"In the job description," I said. "I'm the Guardian of Archers Beach, and you were about to do something really stupid, which, just as a side effect, could've killed us all."

I paused, and added, in case it wasn't clear.

"*You* would have been included in *us all*."

She took a breath that strained the bright ribbons.

"That . . . entity," she said, moving a hand glittering with dark gemstones toward the Enterprise, "has stolen from me."

A word here about the Enterprise. In these parts—these parts being the state of Maine, on the East Coast of the United States—an "enterprise" is a kind of a cross between a junkyard and a flea market. You can find all kinds of *stuff* at an enterprise, from silver teapots to Nixon/Agnew campaign buttons; from slate chalkboards to yellowed lace doilies, to bags of mismatched Legos®.

The Enterprise in Archers Beach also deals in *stuff*: magical stuff, hexed stuff, stuff nobody heard of, stuff nobody wants, and stuff somebody might want 'way too much.

The assertion that the Enterprise had *stolen* from this nice lady didn't particularly shock me. I'd long wondered where the the Enterprise's *stuff* came from. Artie, the *trenvay* whose duty the Enterprise was, could only tell me that "things come in," from time to time, on their own schedule, and with their own ideas. He didn't know where they came from, or necessarily how they arrived. They appeared, was all. Artie's part of the business was to make certain that those things which came in with a purpose or a name attached were delivered to their proper recipients, and the rest were kept—quiet.

But that's getting ahead of things, just a little. There were courtesies to be observed between visitor and Guardian. She should have offered first, being a stranger on my Land, but I could afford to be gracious.

On my Land.

So I bowed, and said easily.

"I'm Kate Archer, Guardian of the Land; heir to Aeronymous, late of the Land of the Flowers."

I got the impression that I'd startled her; that maybe she'd blinked behind those dark glasses. If so, she recovered fast, and produced a very nice bow, indeed.

"I am Annora of Shadowood, in service to the Queen of Daknowyth."

Daknowyth. The Land of Midnight, that would be. Not quite my favorite of the Six Worlds, but it did explain the sunglasses and the concern about the coming dawn.

"So, what exactly did the Enterprise steal from you, and how would blowing it up get whatever it is back?"

Annora bristled.

"I am on the business of my Queen!" she snapped.

"You're on the business of your Queen *on my Land*," I countered. "Since the business of your Queen seems to include *blowing things up* on my Land, I'd—"

"If you had bothered to understand what I was doing," she interrupted sharply, "you would have seen that my intention was to smother everything magic-touched in this area. My . . . items, which are not so touched, would then have been easy to remove."

"That might have been your intention," I said. Admittedly, I'm not very good at spell-craft; for all I knew, her sticky bomb really *had been* only a fire-blanket. But smothering the Enterprise wasn't any better, in the long run, than blowing it sky-high. Worse, really. The Enterprise is used to getting its way.

"Still not a great idea to interfere with the Enterprise."

"Am I to reason with it?" Annora inquired, with a certain amount of justifiable sarcasm.

"No," I said, giving her the point; "that never works. We'll have to reason with the *trenvay*—the spirit of the place—involved . . . . " Which *some*times worked.

"Now, how about—"

"Kate?"

The door to the Enterprise opened, spilling yellow light into the dooryard. Annora hissed and moved a hand; the light dimmed perceptibly as the shadow that was Artie came forward.

"Kate," he said again, ignoring Annora entirely.

"We got a problem."

"I should say *so*!" Annora snapped, and took a deep breath, like she'd remembered where she was, and continued more moderately. "You can cease to have a problem. Merely release them to me."

Artie turned his head, and considered her for a length of time just shy of insulting before turning back to me.

"Who's this?"

"This," I told him, "is Annora of Shadowood, on the business of the Queen of Daknowyth."

"Daknowyth," Artie repeated, like you might say *jellyfish*. He turned back to me.

"What's the trouble?" I asked, to forestall a long detour about Daknowyth, its Queen, and its history, or lack of same, with our very own Changing Land.

"Well," he said, rubbing the back of his neck in a fair semblance of bewilderment. "We got something come in, all right—couple of somethings, if it come to that—but it ain't—*they* ain't—in the usual way."

He paused, and looked me straight in the eye, which was when I knew—*really knew*—just how worried he was.

"An' if we don't get 'em outta there soon, there's no telling what'll happen."

• • • •

THE ENTERPRISE IS ONE smallish three-room shed, and the yard behind it. Every square inch is covered in stuff, and sometimes there's stuff inside the stuff.

Mundane folk—by which I mean people who are magic-blind—mundane folk are the Enterprise's fair game. All summer long, ordinary people walk into the Enterprise, meaning only to stay a couple minutes, ducking in out of the sun, maybe, or just mildly curious. Certainly, they never mean to *buy* anything.

And yet, all summer long, those folks go home with this or that little souvenir that, when questioned, they have only the haziest recollection of having purchased; an ugly little thing, but for some reason, they just can't seem to bring themselves to get rid of it. No one would suggest that there was anything . . . magical . . . in that. Magic wasn't real, after all, and for most of the people in the world—it's just not there. They don't *feel* the energy sparking all around them; they don't *hear* the strange music intended to pull them into a dance they can't hope to survive; they don't *see* the beautiful woman beckoning to them from the wood, and they *certainly* don't follow her off the path.

Magic folk—like me, like Annora of Shadowood, like Artie—magic folk have their own defenses and strategies to answer the lure of the Enterprise. That's not to say that we're not occasionally caught unaware, but the mischief made with us tends to be minor.

No, it's half-magic folk—those who *can* see the weird, but who have no magic of their own—who're in the most danger from the Enterprise—and the risk to them is utterly non-trivial. In most cases, it's life-changing. And not in a good way.

In the old days, they were locked up in attic rooms, or insane asylums. In these enlightened times, we've got drugs for that. The weakest can't prevent magic seeping into them, filling them up until they're no longer, really, themselves.

The strongest make it a policy never to walk down dark alleys, speak to strangers, or to look too nearly into the shadows cast by the street-lights. I don't imagine that they ever sleep sound, but I believe most of them survive.

"The light is increasing," Annora said voice calm, though the Land brought me the sharp stab of her concern.

I sighed.

"Right. Let's get this thing done."

· · · ·

THERE WERE NO MUNDANE customers in the Enterprise this early in the day. That might've been the reason for the extra fizz in the air. Magical being that I am, and Guardian of the Land, too, I could still feel the aisles crowding me, and something a lot like something big, hungry, and with lots of teeth breathing down the back of my neck. The air was alive with whisperings; no words that the ear could actually catch, mind, but you were left with the idea that the Enterprise found you, just faintly, ridiculous.

"What is this place?" Annora asked from behind me. "Why has it not been tamed?"

Behind us, to the left, something . . . growled.

"A little tact might be in order," I said, when the growl had subsided into whispers again.

"Enterprise is old," said Artie, who was bringing up the rear. "Older'n me, and I'm plenty too old. Back when Kate's grandma was a saplin', we got to talking about it one day with the Ol' Forest. Best we could figure, then, was the Enterprise is more gate than anything else, an' most of it's Out Beyond, blowing in the Wind Between the Worlds. Figured that was how stuff come in like it does. I never figured any better. Ain't like it talks to me, really."

"Surely, it will amend itself out of respect for the Guardian," Annora said.

I didn't laugh, but the Enterprise did, lights flickering, and wooden floorboards groaning.

"So, Artie," I said over my shoulder. "Where are these things that just came—"

I stopped, because here they were, of course, and their danger was horrifyingly real.

They were in the second, middle, room of three, as surrounded by the Enterprise as it was possible to be. The room was slightly lower than the first room—three steps down from the floor I stood on, to the floor they stood on, pressed in on all sides by rustic bureaus, spinning wheels, three-legged stools, rocking chairs, and an unstrung harp.

Six youngers, ranging in age from maybe-eight to maybe-twelve, stood in two rows, facing the far wall, the three tallest in front. They were wearing dress native to each of the Six Worlds. Black gown and cloak for the dark Daknowyth miss with the white-as-opal eyes; sky-blue tunic for the pale winged one from Varoth; crimson and black for the fiery redhead from Kashnerot;

waterskins, high boots, and a demi-cloak for the haughty dark-haired youth from Cheobaug; bright silks and a crown of sweet flowers on the head of the child from Sempeki; jeans so old they were white, tennis shoes, and a black t-shirt with a band logo faded 'til I couldn't read it, from our own, the Changing Land.

"*Kids?*" I snapped, and turned to Annora, flinging out a hand in an *explain this* gesture.

"Vestals," she corrected. "Each has accepted the Word of the Queen of Daknowyth and bound themselves to her honor."

"Do their parents know?" I asked.

"In every case, they are kinless," Annora told me with dignity. "The Queen of Daknowyth is not a thief."

"Kate . . . " Artie said from behind me, and I could hear the strain in his voice. "They can't stay here much longer, and I mean *much*. They're all of 'em empty!"

Turning back, I saw what he meant.

The room was dim; expectable, given the hour and the fact that the Enterprise was poorly lit by design.

The kids, though—the kids were standing in a spotlight of pearly light, each casting a shadow of lambent silver. I realized then that I was looking at innocence; at purity, if you'll allow it. None of them possessed the least shred of magic. All of them could see the weird; taste it; hear it. Their one defense was their virtue—and that wasn't going to be enough.

Magic, in case I forgot to say earlier, abhors a vacuum. It will strive to fill any empty vessel with itself. The Enterprise, being old in guile and in magic, desired nothing more than to fill each of those kids up with itself, and possess them, utterly.

The Land trembled with the Enterprise's lust, and I started to feel a little sick. No time for that now. *Now*, I looked deeper, and—yes; there were dark flares and flashes just beyond that nimbus of purity, chewing away at the edges, but not, I noticed, too quickly. The Enterprise was enjoying this game, and had a mind to stretch it out.

"That will do!" Annora stepped forward, and I dropped back a step to let her have a full view of the situation.

"These are not yours to take!" she cried, power thrumming in her voice. "These are the Vestals of Midnight. They are under the shield of the Queen of Daknowyth, which I, her appointed representative, now extend!"

That quick, something black, supple and complex flowed out and over the room, drifting like a sweet cloud over the heads of the six kids. It was, I saw, intended to envelope them, like armor, whereupon they could be led out of the center of the Enterprise's ravenous web.

Except, it never settled.

The . . . things that had been gnawing at the edge of the circle of light abruptly merged into a blare of oily lightning, stabbing straight into the heart of the cloud.

Thunder boomed. Sparks flew. The furniture lunged forward, legs clattering like hooves on the old wooden floor.

The red-haired boy yelled and thrust out a hand, catching a flying sugar bowl and throwing it at a book that was flapping toward them like a raven.

The kid from the Changing Land kicked out, in perfect form, smacking a charging spinning wheel with the flat of her sneaker, sending it crashing back into a bookcase filled with ugly knick-knacks.

"Hey!" Artie yelled. "You be careful! Them things is worth money!"

In the doorway, Annora gestured. I felt power surge, saw a second iteration of the black shield flow into being—only to be torn to shreds by the Enterprise's outrage.

It was only a matter of seconds before things started breaking, and there was no assurance that the kids would survive the battle of wills.

On the other hand, Annora *was* drawing the Enterprise's fire.

I reached to the Land, and through it spoke directly to the kids. "Let's go! Run! This way!"

They tried. The girl from the Changing Land and the boy from the Land of Wave and Water each grabbed the hands of the two kids nearest them and dragged them forward. The first three steps were fine—not a run, but brisk enough—the fourth step was like they were walking through mud; the fifth step—well, the Changing Land kid managed a fifth step, but none of the rest of them did.

The Enterprise *roared*.

Dust blew up in a swirling plume, crockery broke, a stool danced a tango across the floor, slammed into a rocking chair, and knocked it onto its back.

Annora groaned. I could see her struggling to raise yet another wave of energy, but the Enterprise had its dander up, now; the air so thick with malice it was barely possible to breathe.

"She's gonna blow!" Artie yelled, and I heard boots pounding on the floor behind me.

I reached to the Land, drew power into my bones, and Spoke with Words of fire.

"That's enough."

The dust devil congealed and fell to the floor with an audible thump.

The furniture froze in place.

The roaring stopped.

In the abrupt silence, one last piece of crockery fell off of a shelf and broke, quietly, on a musty hooked rug.

Beside me, Annora of Shadowood drew in a very, *very* long breath.

I could feel the weight of the Enterprise's attention, focused directly on me; and it wasn't the best feeling I'd had in my life. I felt the whole power of the Land singing in my blood, potent, alive, strong. I *was* Archers Beach, and my Word here was law.

"Release the virgins," I said. "Do it now."

The Enterprise hesitated. It . . . *growled*.

Oh, yeah?

"Are you," I asked, gently; there was no need, after all, to shout; "going to make me come down there?"

The growl . . . died. The kid from the Changing Land shouted and rushed forward, still holding onto the hands of the kids from Sempeki and Kashnerot. Behind them came the other three.

I swung back from the doorway, they jumped up the stairs, and I waved them on—

"Go! Outside! Annora!"

But Annora was already moving, sweeping them ahead of her, out of the Enterprise, into the dawnlight.

Me, I stood there a second longer, listening to the Enterprise brood.

"I'll come back," I said. "When I do, we'll talk about your role in the Age of Science."

The Enterprise . . . whimpered.

"It'll be fun," I told it, and turned on my heel and went away.

• • • •

ANNORA WAS STANDING beneath the big tree at the edge
of the Enterprise's dooryard, surrounded by the Midnight Vestals.
Artie stood a little apart, hands twisting together.

"Kate." He started forward. I paused.

"How's the weather?" he asked me, jerking his head toward the
Enterprise.

"Subdued. I'll be back to do some work. In the meantime,
maybe you'd better clean up."

He grimaced.

"Some of that stuff was actual antiques," he said, half-accusing.

"So now the stuff that's left is worth more," I said, and moved
on.

The Land showed me Artie standing behind me, indecisive for
a moment. Then he squared his shoulders and walked into the
Enterprise, closing the door behind him.

Annora had pulled her hood over her face. Right. It was dawn.
Time for her to go.

Just one more thing, though.

"The Vestals of Midnight hold the Queen of Daknowyth's
honor?" I said.

She bowed.

"For thirteen years, they do. At the end of their service, they
are returned to their native Lands, provided with all and every
comfort."

I turned to look at the kids; met the eyes of the Changing Land
girl.

"You good with this?" I asked her.

"I'm good," she answered. And, like she felt maybe that was a little brief, added, "We'll have tutors. Three meals a day. Better'n what I got now. An' nobody'll touch us, on account we belong to the Queen."

"And by the time we are released to our own lives again," the boy from Cheobaug added, grimly, "no one will be *able* to touch us."

Kinless, Annora had said.

I nodded.

"Come see me," I said, to them all. "When your service is done."

"I'll do that, ma'am," said the girl from the Changing Land; the others murmuring their promises behind her.

The child from Sempeki stepped forward, bowing and offering the flower crown.

I bent my head gravely, and felt it settled gently on my hair.

The child stepped back, and I raised my head to look at the six of them, shining sweet and pure in the growing light.

"I regret that you were ever in danger on my Land," I said, which was nothing more than the plain truth. "And I salute your valor and your loyalty to each other."

I stepped back, and glanced at Annora.

"There's no Gate here, anymore."

"That is of no concern," she said calmly, "we ride upon the back of the winds."

Unexpectedly, she bowed, much lower than she needed to do.

"The Queen will be told of your service to Daknowyth, Kate Archer. You have also my thanks. Use my name as your own."

"Thank you," I said, with no intention of *ever* invoking *that* debt.

"Yes," she said, and opened her arms.

"To me," she said, and the kids moved in close, taking shelter in the expanding shadow of her cloak, until . . .

I stood alone in the dawn-light, the power of the Land singing in my blood.

Wolf in the Wind

Chapter One
Cael

"**W**hat took you so long? It coulda killed the whole town!"
Cael opened the door, and slid out of the truck. Oscar, in the passenger seat, watched attentively, mistrustful of the woman with her loud voice. He would have caught the smell of fear as clearly as Cael did.

The woman was blocking access to Storage Unit Number L9, holding a broom across her chest in a two-handed grip. Behind her, the roll-up door was rolled down.

"You didn't let it out, did you?" Cael asked, walking softly forward.

The woman wore an orange plastic jacket, with a picture of a *glashtyn* rising from the water. "Swamp Thing Storage" was stitched on the right breast; "Manager" on the left. Cael's own jacket carried the seal of the town of Archers Beach, "Animal Control" above it, and his name, "C. Wolfe," below.

"Didn't let what out?" the manager asked, frowning.

"The snake," Cael said. "It couldn't have killed anyone, if it was confined in the—unit."

"Wise ass," the woman snapped. "You dawdle your way down here, and now you're making jokes?"

It hadn't been a joke, but Cael had learned not to correct such statements, or to protest that he had been at another job when her call had come in, which he had been constrained to finish first. Fear made time run faster, and if, indeed, the captive was as dangerous as she represented, the manager had done well to keep it confined.

"Please stand aside," he said now, walking past, and bending down to grab the handle of the roll-up door. He didn't want her in the line of a rush, or a discharge.

"What?"

Fingers around the door handle, he turned his head to look up at her.

"Stand aside," he repeated. "You don't wish to be hurt."

"Right," she said, and hastily withdrew, stopping with her back against the animal control truck.

Cael nodded, spinning to the right as he threw the door up—and waited.

Nothing happened. There was no odor of brimstone, nor stink of poison. He sensed no enmity. Indeed, he sensed only the most minor tingle of life—slow, cool life.

"Kill it!" shouted the manager behind him. "What are you waiting for?"

Cael frowned. The interior of Unit L9 was crammed with large pieces of furniture, boxes were piled near the front, and a leather footstool had been placed atop the pile nearest the door.

On the footstool, curled in a puddle of late September sunlight that had found its way into the unit through the window in the roof—was a snake.

A very sleepy, contented snake.

"Kill it!" the manager snarled into his ear.

Cael turned to her.

"Why?" he asked, genuinely puzzled. "It's sleeping, and it is harmless."

"It's a snake!"

"Yes," Cael said patiently. "It is a snake. A northern water snake. It is harmless—no. It is better than harmless. It eats vermin. Its presence has been preventing mice from eating the boxes and fouling the furniture."

"A—look, you, I know a cottonmouth when I see one! They're mean-tempered and they're poisonous."

Cael frowned. He had studied hard to learn all the creatures of this Land that he served. There were, however, other Lands, and other creatures, of which he was ignorant.

He tipped his head, considering that last thought. While it was true that there were other Lands, snakes were much alike, wherever they were found. They did not travel far, save by accident, or the intent of those other than themselves. Unless this snake had arrived with the rest of the storage bay's furnishings, it was what it appeared to be—a northern water snake.

On the footstool, the snake moved, light glinting along its scales. Its head rose.

Cael reached for his link to this, his own, Land. Through it, he murmured to the snake.

"Tell me true: are you of this Land?"

"Yessss . . ." the snake answered, head moving slightly, its thoughts drugged with warmth.

"Lie easy," Cael cautioned it. "There is one here who calls your life forfeit; she believes you to be a poisoner."

There came an unsteady hiss, as if the snake was laughing, then it spoke, less drowsy now.

"That's not unjust; my mouth's a weapon, but my bite's for mice and vermin."

A pause.

"Though I'll make an exception, if my life's on the line."

"Yes," said Cael. "Lie easy and hide your teeth. I will need to move you, but I will preserve your life."

"'preciate it," said the snake, and lowered its head.

"Why haven't you killed it?" The manager's voice was shaking. "It's a cottonmouth."

"There are no cottonmouths here," Cael said, projecting absolute certainty.

He felt the manager's fear ease, somewhat. She went so far as to smile at him.

"Fine; it's not poisonous," she said agreeably. "Kill it anyway."

"No," Cael said, and held up a hand. "I will remove it. It is a useful creature in its proper place."

"Which ain't a storage bin!"

"Precisely. I will remove it to its proper place. Stand away."

"You ain't half a smart-mouth, are ya?"

"I lack the appropriate measuring stick," he told her. "Stand away; I will not have you harming this creature."

The manager stared, lips parted, face white with rage. She stepped forward, and he heard Oscar growl from the front seat of the truck. Cael made another small request from the Land.

The manager stopped, as if rooted, drew in a shaky breath, and used the broom to point at the drowsy reptile.

"Get that thing out of here," she said, voice raspy. "If you wanna take it home and keep it for a pet, that's all right by me. It's got no place in my storage park, understand me?"

"Yes," said Cael, patiently. "I understand. Please stand back. I will bring a container from the truck, and remove the snake."

She eyed him, and he clearly saw her desire to end the innocent life with her broom.

"Where you taking it?" she asked.

"To a safe place," Cael said evenly, and walked to the back of the truck.

• • • •

THE SNAKE SLITHERED out of the box at swamp side.

"Fare well," Cael told it. "Perhaps do not go into the storage units again. You might not be so lucky twice."

The snake paused, and lifted its head, cold eyes meeting Cael's gaze.

"There's some good eatin' over there," it commented.

"Is dinner worth your life?" Cael asked.

It moved its head, and the land brought Cael the impression of a sigh.

"Guess not." It paused. "You don't mind my askin', deah, what d'you happen to be, zackly?"

"I am an animal control officer."

The snake waited. Cael waited.

The snake turned and flowed across the mud, and down into a murky pool.

Cael sighed and got to his feet.

• • • •

HE PULLED THE TRUCK into the garage, opened the door and slid out, clipboard in hand, Oscar behind him.

It took only a moment to open the back of the truck and make his inventory, then he locked up and headed for the office, Oscar at his knee.

"Good evening, John," he said, putting his clipboard on Karen's desk. He went to the time clock hanging on the wall, pulled his card out of its slot, slid it into the machine's maw.

KLUNG!

He removed the card, slotted it, then turned to face John, who oversaw his work here. John was not a bad man, by Cael's measuring. He had no personal tie to the Land, but that could be said of most of the people who lived within the boundaries of Archers Beach. Despite that deficiency, he had a genuine care for the creatures of the Land. John had once been what Cael was—an animal control officer—before his supervisor had stepped back from her duty, and John had been "kicked upstairs," as he said it.

That was the circumstance that had allowed Cael to take up the active care of the creatures of Archers Beach, while John sat inside at a desk, doing paperwork, negotiating with those above him in the town administration.

And taking complaints.

"Made yourself a lifelong friend with Jerri Evans over there at the storage factory," John said now.

Cael sighed, genuinely grieved.

"I am sorry that she called you," he said.

"Comes to that, so'm I," John said. He glanced down and held a hand out. Oscar being a gentleman who knew what rank required of him, he thrust his nose into John's palm, *hoofed* gently and wagged his tail.

John smiled slightly, some of the tension going out of his shoulders.

"Thanks, Oscar," he said, and looked back at Cael.

"You get that snake situated?"

"I returned it to the marsh," Cael said. "I—think it will not venture into the storage rooms again."

"Better not, if it values its life," John said. "Jerri Evans tells me she'll kill the next snake she sees on her property, don't care what kind, the only good snake being, according to her, a dead one."

"The snake today," Cael said. "It was not—any more dangerous than another snake. Not poisonous. Not a—cottonmouth." He looked to John.

"What *is* a cottonmouth?"

"A water snake, down Away. Sometimes you'll hear 'em called water moccasins. Sooner bite either of us than bother to swim away. Similar markin's to your northern water snake, which Jerri tells me you told her is what today's player was."

"Yes."

John looked thoughtful.

"Not that there's any snake that isn't dangerous, come down to facts. Filthy mouths. You get bit, the infection'll be enough to kill you if you don't get help quick."

"Yes," Cael said again.

"So that's me telling you to be careful around snakes," John said. Cael looked at him in surprise.

"Of course," he said. "A snake cannot go against its nature."

"Right you are, and you did right, moving today's back where it belonged. Now—" John sighed, and rubbed the back of his neck.

Cael waited. Oscar leaned against his knee.

"Jerri tells me you were too long answering the call, and gave her some attitude when you did get there."

Cael frowned.

John sighed.

"So, where were you before you went to see Jerri?"

Cael's face cleared.

"I was half-way up a tree."

John blinked.

"Pretty Boots got out again?"

Pretty Boots was not the true-name of the cat to whom Mrs. Angela Newton owed fealty, but that was to be expected; cats rarely shared their true-names. What was . . . distressing was that Pretty Boots made sport of her servant. Three times in the last two weeks, Cael had been called to bring Pretty Boots out of a tree. Today, he had remonstrated with her, trying to instill in her a sense of the obligations attached to her station.

Pretty Boots had tried to scratch him.

But none of this was John's concern.

"Pretty Boots did get out again," he said. "Mrs. Newton says that she unlatched the screen door with her paw."

"Don't doubt it; damn' cat's an escape artist." John shook his head. "'fraid we're gonna have to downgrade Mrs. Newton's calls to 'respond at leisure.'"

Cael blinked, thinking of the elder lady's face today when he returned the cat to her—pale and grateful to him for his service, her cheeks damp with tears.

"Mrs. Newton can scarcely climb the tree herself," he objected.

The Land brought him the taste of John's distress—and the metallic tang of determination.

"Nope, she can't. But she's taking up too much of a limited resource—that's your time—so she's gonna have to wait 'til after you shift snakes outta storage pods, and round up your various strays. You got nothing else on the list, then you see to Pretty Boots."

This, thought Cael, was not a practicable solution. There had been nothing else on the list when Mrs. Newton's call came in today. He did not say this to John, however. Clearly, a solution had to be found for Pretty Boots, but that solving surely fell within Cael's honor as *trenvay*—a servant of the Land.

"Very well," he said.

John gave him a stare. John was a man of determination and courage, and the stare might have produced a tremor in the heart of a man.

But not in the heart of a wolf.

"Maybe you don't know who lives across from Mrs. Newton," John said, "so I'll tell you. Avis Marcant. You know, the councilor who wants you fired so her son-in-law can get put into your job?"

"Yes," Cael said, and did not add that the councilor also failed to approve of his appearance, and the place of his birth, as recorded on his birth certificate.

"There's a face says *Maine*," he had heard her say to her henchwoman, Bethany Miller, who had laughed lightly and answered, pretty voice full of malice, "Spends a lot of time out in the sun, don't he?"

He might have said to John that anything he did or did not do in order to please or placate Avis Marcant was doomed to fall short of hope—but he did not. John's position also depended on the whim of this petty lady. Cael owed nothing to her, but he did owe duty to John.

"I will remember," he said now, and Oscar thumped his tail on the floor, jaws parting in a particularly charming grin.

John's shoulders relaxed a little more, and he smiled, very slightly.

"Comedians," he said, and slid off the desk to his feet. "Go on along home, the both of you. You keep him outta trouble, Oscar."

The dog thumped his tail again. Cael smiled and turned toward the door.

Chapter Two
Kate

I never could figure out how I'd come to be on The Committee—that's the Fun Country Leaseback Committee to you. According to Jess Robard, I was on it because I was the owner-operator of one of the Named Rides, and therefore some kind of carny royalty. I didn't buy it, and said so, several times, loudly—but here I was, anyway—committee fodder.

God, I hate committees.

According to Jess, that was a feature.

"Kept everybody on point and focused, that's what," she'd told me, after the first meeting. "Service to the community, that's what you are, Kate Archer."

Yeah, some service. On the other hand, it wasn't like I was new to being of service to the community, being the Guardian of the Land known as Archers Beach. Not that the community, most of 'em, knew it—just those who happened to be tied to odd little bits of land, water, marsh; to this or that tree, or enterprise. The *trenvay*, those folks were called—minor magic users, and general Others. The rest of the community of Archers Beach—plain human folk—didn't much believe in magic, which was their protection, if not their guarantee of safety.

So, I'd gone to the meeting, and now I was walking back home from the library, where the body of the committee barely fit into the public meeting room, and pretty much overwhelmed the little window air conditioner.

It was warm for late September, clear blue skies and bright sun. The overnight would be crisp enough to require a sweatshirt or long-sleeved sweater for an evening walk through town, and something a little more for the beach. The Atlantic Ocean was still warm, but the breeze was foretelling winter.

Despite the weather, there weren't many people in town. Fun Country had closed for the season, and Management, down in New Jersey, had refused to consider staying open 'til Columbus Day, even just on weekends. Which was completely in character for Management, and not one of owner-operators in the park ought to have been shocked, horrified, or pissed off by their decision, but—they were. At least, some of them were, myself not included. I hadn't thought it worth asking, truly, but the rest had been riding high on the victory of having bought the park and saved it from being condofied. Given that they'd already pulled off one miracle, why not shoot for two?

I hit the corner of Archer Avenue, waved to Lisa, who was serving up pizza slices to three teenage boys with skateboards under their arms, and turned right, toward the ocean.

There were maybe a dozen people in Fountain Circle, some occupying tables, some sitting on the wide stone edge of the fountain, chatting, or just taking in the day. Overhead, the flags fluttered noisily in the landside breeze.

To my right, there was Fun Country, gate locked; rides, games, and food counters all wrapped up and sealed for the winter. Just inside, to the left, the first ride everybody saw when they came through the open gate, was the Fantasy Menagerie Carousel, the oldest ride in the park, Kate Archer, owner-operator.

I walked up to the gate and wrapped my fingers around a warm metal bar, leaning in to look down Baxter Avenue. To my left, just behind the carousel, Summer's Wheel was naked metal spokes; the gondolas had been removed, wrapped in blue tarp, and lined up beneath. Down a little further, the Samurai was swathed in the same blue weatherproofing, the doors to the Oriental Fun House boarded up. The game kiosks down the center of the avenue were shuttered, just like the fortune-telling booth, the t-shirt shop, and Tony Lee's Chinese Food.

A breeze came up, smelling wistfully of egg rolls, and halfheartedly lifted a handful of dust into a swirl. The edge of the tarp covering the Samurai flapped in complaint, and the breeze died, leaving the dust scattered across the tarmac.

I sighed and turned away, my eyes going with a kind of involuntary dread to the commotion across the Circle.

In the recent past—by which I mean, the Season that had ended on Labor Day—there had been a midway across the Circle—games of skill and chance, a climbing wall, food vendors, henna artists, and all that sort of thing. It had been noisy, it had been crowded, it had made money for Management down in Jersey . . .

But not *enough* money.

Management had to protect its bottom line; that's what Management *does*, after all.

So, long story short, Management sold the midway to the highest bidder, which happened to be a new-made Boston-based LLC with condos in its eye, and it wasn't letting the smallest blade of grass get between its toes.

The midway had barely closed for the Season when the first crews arrived and began taking down the games, the booths, and the climbing wall. Two days after, the big equipment arrived on the backs of haulers, and they'd commenced in to digging.

Now, where the games and concessions had been, there was—a hole. Not much of a hole, yet, but at the rate the machines were working, it wouldn't be long before we were helping Chinamen climb up over the lip.

I shook my head, turned aside and went past the carousel, following the fence to the sidewalk's end, and on some more, over dry sand to wet, down to the very edge of the ocean.

I stood for a minute, looking out over the water. Tide was coming in; I took a deep breath, tasting brine, and sighed it out. To my left was the Pier. I could hear a sound check going on inside of Neptune's, at the very end of the boardwalk. Being a locally owned bar and dance club, Neptune's was taking advantage of every nice day and evening that September delivered, though it, too, would be closed by mid-October, when the tourists stopped coming in, and the townie traffic wasn't enough to keep the lights on.

Well. I smiled at the ocean, turned and walked under the Pier, along the water line, heading north, up the beach toward the old house on Dube Street, the waves crashing companionably on my right hand.

I emerged from the shadow of the Pier into the late afternoon sunshine, thinking about the hole in the ground where the midway used to be. Change . . . well, it *was* change. They don't call us the Changing Land for nothing. It's our greatest strength—and our greatest weakness.

Even though it was a necessary part of how the world operated—I didn't always care for change.

Up ahead, the waves charged the shore, foam flying like the manes of fey horses, each crash merging with the other, until there was one, continuous sound of the sea meeting the land, and—

A wave flew toward the shore, directly toward me, longer and taller than its comrades, striking with a boom that was all its own, engulfing me, then lifting me up, into arms that were solid, strong, and warm.

"Hey!" I shouted, part indignation, part laughter, and looked down into a big, brown face, black eyes bright as a moonlit night under black brows; broad nose, and a generous mouth, just now grinning in mischief.

"Hey, yourself," he answered. "Gotta be careful, walking the water's edge with the tide comin' in."

"Or else what?" I asked him, resting my hands on warm, broad shoulders.

"Else you'll get wet."

I was not, I noticed, wet. Nor was Borgan.

"I'm fairly warned," I said. "You gonna put me down or not?"

His face turned thoughtful.

"I could go either way," he said, "though I'm thinking you'll want to be set down."

The truth of the matter was that I wasn't all *that* eager to be set down. All things in their time, as they say, and given that, I hadn't given the man his proper welcome after our long separation of, oh—call it eight hours.

I bent my head to kiss him—one of my new favorite pastimes is kissing Borgan, right enough, but after that, it was bending *down* to kiss Borgan, which is only possible if I'm standing three steps up and he's on the sidewalk, or—

He was holding me against his shoulder, my feet 'way off the ground.

It was a thorough kiss, appropriate to the occasion of our reunion. It ended naturally; I sighed, and Borgan did, and I touched his cheek softly.

"Dinner and dancing at my place?" I asked.

"Sounds good," he answered, and bent to set me on my feet.

• • • •

CAEL WAS SITTING ON the front steps when we got to the house on Dube Street. He was barefoot, wearing a pair of khaki cargo shorts and a bright red shirt with a large gold foil design on the front, that might've equally been a flower or a bird. Oscar's head was on his knee, the dog's expression one of uncomplicated bliss, as Cael stroked his nose and head.

They both looked up as we approached, and Cael bowed his head, which I could *not* break him of, though he had finally managed to overcome his good up-bringing and—mostly—address me as "Kate," rather than "my lady."

By Cael's lights, Borgan was my consort, but not his lord, so the only thing he'd needed to be weaned from there was "sir."

"Good evening," he said now. "Kate. Borgan."

"Evening," I answered, and Borgan did, too, just like neither of us was concerned that Cael's presence would alter our pleasant evening plans.

Cael lived in the former rental unit at my back, just half-a-dozen steps from the bottom of the stairs. That particular arrangement was a compromise. I thought Cael and Oscar should have their own place, and Cael thought that his lady's Master of Hounds ought to be near to her hand, as she had no others to serve her. Not even pointing out that I had the entire Land of Archers Beach to serve me, not to mention the Lord of the Gulf of Maine holding an interest, had managed to shake him loose of the concept that no one could serve Lady Aeronymous—that being how I was styled in the land of my birth—more fitly than himself.

So, Cael lived in the studio, and had access to the house; and I lived in the house where I'd grown up, free to entertain my consort whenever and however I liked. Not that Cael was judgmental—he left that to Breccia.

"What can I do for you?" I asked now, because there was no use putting the thing off.

"I would like to speak to the Lady Breccia," Cael answered. "I hope that she will assist me in unknotting a vexatious difficulty with one of her own."

Breccia's own being feline. I shrugged.

"Sure," I said. "Come on up and we'll see if her ladyship's receiving."

• • • •

BRECCIA LIKED CAEL, despite the whole cat/dog thing, so it wasn't a big surprise to find her strolling across the kitchen toward us when we came through the door.

Cael glanced at Oscar, who recused himself, wandering over to the French doors overlooking the sparkling Atlantic Ocean, and sprawling in a splash of sun.

Cael dropped to one knee, and bowed his head, squinting his eyes in a cat smile.

"My lady," he said softly. "You honor me with your radiant presence."

Breccia continued forward, stropped herself along his knee, and sat facing him. She squinted her eyes.

"Everything that is gracious," Cael murmured.

Borgan at my back, I walked lightly around both of them and the kitchen table to reach the fridge.

"Ale?" I murmured.

"Sounds fine," he answered, and took the bottle I handed out to him. I got my own bottle, and leaned next to him against the kitchen counter, prepared to witness the negotiations.

"I bring news of one of my lady's kindred. It is not for me to judge such a one, but I feel that her behavior is . . . unworthy." Cael paused and shrugged lightly. "This may of course be because my understanding of things feline is . . . at fault."

Breccia squinted her eyes again, ceding the point and inviting him to go on.

"There is one who allows herself to be known as Pretty Boots. She maintains a modest establishment on Burdette Street, supported by an elderly and devoted servant. In former days, she would betimes leave the house to walk up and down the town. Since attaining a certain age and grace, she became less likely to exercise her rights in this way—until recently."

He paused, head bowed slightly, apparently awaiting whatever question Breccia might have.

I had a sip from my bottle. Borgan adjusted his lean against the counter so that his hip touched mine.

Breccia flicked an ear.

"Yes," Cael said. "Recently Pretty Boots has taken to letting herself out of the house and climbing the tree adjacent to her residence. Her servant has begged her to recall her station, to no avail. In my duty as Animal Control Officer, I have five times been called to physically extract her from the tree and return her to the care of her servant, who has been more distressed in each succeeding instance. Today, I took it upon myself to remonstrate with Pretty Boots, whereupon—she scratched me."

I sent a gentle query to the Land, which assured me that the scratch had been healed a bare moment after it had been received, which was no more than I had expected.

Breccia produced another ear-flick. Cael sighed.

"I am aware that it was unsubtle, but I am concerned for the servant, who is, as I have said, elderly, and daily made distraught by what seems to me, a most fallible wolf, her liege's willful neglect of her obligations."

He paused for a breath, and continued without waiting for a sign from Breccia.

"The situation has been made more desperate, as my supervisor today announced a new order to my duties: If I am called to succor Pretty Boots, I answer that call last. And, if the events of the day conspire so that I do not reach the last item before it is time for me to give over duty for the night, then I am to ignore the call entirely."

Breccia's tail snapped—to the right, to the left. And stopped, laid out on the floor behind her as straight as a ruler, and as stiff.

I drank off my ale and put the empty on the counter behind me.

Breccia still hadn't moved, and I was getting the idea that she wasn't half pissed off.

Cael must've thought so, too, because he dropped his head, keeping his eyes aimed at the floor.

"Lady Breccia, I am afraid for the old servant. Her heart may break beneath this show of contempt from one she has served so long. But more, I fear for Pretty Boots, that she has become lost to honor, and to all knowledge of her obligations."

Wow.

I realized I was holding my breath, and held it some more. Next to me, Borgan was doing the same.

Breccia looked like she was made out of the same rock as her chosen name.

Just when I felt like the choice was between breathing and fainting, Breccia stood. She stretched high, back humping, tail rising to describe a question mark. She strolled to the front door, and looked over her shoulder at Cael.

"Of course, my lady," Cael murmured, and came lightly to his feet. "Oscar will accompany us," he added, but Breccia had already turned her head away, such petty arrangements being beneath her.

"Why don't we all go?" said Borgan; his voice a rumble against my side. I turned my head around and looked up into his face.

"Sure," I said, "why not? It's a nice night for a walk."

Chapter Three
Kate

It *was* a nice night for a walk. I'd pulled on my denim jacket, and Borgan had rolled down his shirt sleeves. Cael hadn't bothered with long pants, jacket, or shoes. Breccia rode on his left shoulder, erect as a warrior princess in her chariot, and Oscar ambled along at his right knee.

"Best laid plans," I muttered to Borgan, who looked down with a half-smile on his face.

"Walk before's supposed to give you an appetite," he commented.

"That's *dinner*," I told him, sternly.

"Haven't had dinner yet, have we?"

I didn't dignify that with an answer, and anyway, here we were on Burdette Street, hard by a tidy little town cottage, in need of some cosmetics: a coat of paint, new shutters, maybe a new roof and she'd be good as could be.

There was a driveway on the right, mostly filled by an oldish Oldsmobile station wagon parked nose out. On the left of the house was a tiny square of land, entirely taken up by a large maple tree.

"Pretty Boots' tree?" I asked the night, and Cael nodded, as Breccia flowed down him like a jaguar down a cliff, and walked up the three wooden steps to the front door.

Oscar at heel, Cael followed her, and pressed the bell.

Borgan and I stayed behind on the sidewalk, and I felt the kiss of a briny breeze against my cheek, which was Borgan suggesting to anybody who happened to be watching that we weren't there.

A minute passed, dawdling. Then another. I felt Borgan shift beside me, like he was thinking about maybe stepping up and putting his hand on the knob—but just about then, the door *did* open and a tall spare lady with crystal white hair stood framed there, her attention fixed on Cael.

My attention was on Breccia, who casually strolled over the stoop and into the house like she owned the place. I might have twitched. Borgan put his arm around my waist, and I leaned into the solid warmth of him.

The lady hesitated a moment, glanced down, got a look at Oscar, and then looked back up.

"Why, Mr. Wolfe, what a surprise! Surely you don't work this late!"

"I am off-duty now," Cael told her. "I was thinking of you and of Pretty Boots and hoped that it would be all right if I came to ask after you."

"That's very kind. We're both fine. Just had our dinners and settling down to watch a little television, you know. Now that you're here, I have a chance to thank you for your patience and your skill in fetching Bootsy out of that tree. Honestly, I don't know what's gotten into her lately. Do you think I ought to take her to the vet?"

There was a little niggle in the back of my head, a suggestion that maybe I should look up, and over, where—

"Borgan," I said softly. "There's something *in* that tree."

"Any special kinda something?"

"It's . . . " I reached to the Land and asked a favor. Obligingly, it sharpened my vision, so that I could see into the branches, and the shadows near the bole, but by that time, I hardly needed the boost. Other senses were tingling, and I knew damn' well what it was.

"Willie wisp," I told Borgan.

There was a little silence, strongly seasoned with surprise. Up on the stoop, Cael and Mrs. Newton were running out of mutual admiration. She moved back a little, easing the door forward.

"Like to know what one of them's doing here," Borgan said finally, tipping his head back and staring up into the tree. "Being as the Wise cut us off."

"They say," I answered.

Cael gave Mrs. Newton a gallant little bow and a smile. He glanced down at Oscar, and the two of them turned.

Mrs. Newton smiled, nodded, and turned back into the house, the door swinging shut behind her.

Just before it closed, a white, orange and black streak flashed between door and jamb, flowed down the steps and was waiting on the sidewalk when Cael and Oscar reached it.

Cael nodded, and joined us at the end of the driveway, where he went down on one knee, offering his shoulder to Breccia, who hesitated, then leapt, landing lightly, and sticking her nose in his ear.

He rose, a frown between his brows.

"My lady Breccia would have us know that the house-tree harbors a—pest normally below the notice of Pretty Boots. However, this pest is of a kind that is particularly dangerous to her servant, therefore Pretty Boots at first tried to drive it away. When it ran, but returned, she changed her tactic, and now seeks to kill it. Today, it stung her. She was in pain from this wound when I took her off her branch. She tried to bear me with patience, but found me too much for her temper."

He paused, lips twitching.

"Pretty Boots offers an apology and hopes that my own wound does not hinder me in my duty."

"Well," I said. "Turns out Pretty Boots is right. There's a willie wisp in that tree—" I raised my arm to point—and lowered it.

"Which isn't there, now," I finished.

"Which matches up with young Bootsy's story," Borgan said. "It runs away, and comes back."

I saw a flicker of white out of the corner of my eye, which might've been Mrs. Newton looking out her window at Cael and Oscar standing at the end of her drive, a circumstance that might be worrying to an elderly lady living alone.

"Let's move on," I said, turning back the way we'd come. Cael, Breccia on his shoulder and Oscar at his knee, strolled with us.

"It is true that I have not detected any spoor," he said slowly. "And I swear to you, My Lady, I have been up that tree *many* times."

"Kate," I said absently. "I believe you."

Given that I *did* believe him, I, as the Archer of Archers Beach, or more specifically, the Guardian of the Land of Archers Beach, had a problem.

On the one hand, Pretty Boots had been right—willie wisps are vermin, powered by malice, and always hungry. While they aren't smart, they *are* cunning, especially in the matter of feeding themselves, and that was where this got to be my problem. As Guardian, it was my duty to protect the Land and those it nurtured. Angela Newton fell into that last category, and she was a willie wisp banquet.

See, willies . . . are from Away. 'way Away. They're native to Sempeki, also known as the Land of the Flowers. What they eat there are the leftovers from spells and workings and the odd battle of wills—elemental fragments, call them. What they eat here in our very own Changing Land are—memories, the older, the better. A woman in her late sixties, early seventies, was likely to have a whole lot of memories.

"How'd it get here?" Borgan asked again.

"Maybe it got caught on the wrong side when the Gate closed," I said, sounding cranky to myself. "Who counts willie wisps to make sure none're missing?"

"Point."

"Regardless of *how* it is here, it is hunting," Cael said, practically. "It has seen a feast from which it must eat." He stopped, and looked over his shoulder in the direction of Mrs. Newton's house. "Pretty Boots is valiant, but valor alone is not enough for this. I will wait, and dispatch it when it returns."

"Might've gotten scared off by all the attention," Borgan said, but not like he believed it.

"Willie wisps aren't clever," I said. "If this one's been here since the Gate closed, it's hungry—well, they always are. But they don't have any natural predators here, and Mrs. Newton's got to be awfully tempting. I don't like her chances, even with Pretty Boots to guard her."

I looked at Breccia.

"How *is* Pretty Boots, by the way? A willie sting can go bad, if it's not cleaned."

The Land brought me an image of Breccia licking the swollen white paw of a pudgy gray short-hair, and a flutter along nerves that I knew well. The Land had helped Breccia heal Pretty Boots. I sighed in relief.

"Pretty soon you won't need me," I said, "and I'll retire to Florida."

Breccia flicked her ears, and stared over my head.

"Right." I looked at Cael.

"Are you taking this on?" I asked him. "What about work tomorrow?"

"I will go to work tomorrow," he assured me. "The willie wisp will come again, tonight. It knows it wounded the house's protector, and in the dark it has an advantage."

I hesitated, but, hell, he was a grown man, and furthermore, he was familiar with the prey. In the Land of the Flowers, a child can dispatch a willie wisp with a single Word. It wasn't like Cael was going to be shooting a gun, unsheathing a knife, or even bringing his staff into play. One Word, and it would be over.

"Go for it," I told him, like he needed my permission. "What about Oscar?"

He tipped his head, considering.

"Borgan," he said gently. "Will you allow Lady Breccia to ride?"

"Sure thing," said Borgan, and put a hand on Cael's shoulder, so Breccia could walk across the bridge of his arm and settle on his shoulder.

Cael sank to one knee, and looked into Oscar's eyes.

"You will guard Kate this evening, while I track this quarry. The terrain is unfriendly to you, else you would be at my side, as always you are. Our reunion on the morrow will gladden us both."

Oscar didn't like it. He whined, and put his paw on Cael's thigh. In the end, though, he stood and came to my side.

"That's all right, then," I said, reaching down to fondle one floppy ear. "See you tomorrow, Cael."

"Yes," he said, and turned away, walking swiftly on bare, silent feet.

I turned to Borgan.

"Still up for dinner and dancing?"

He looked down at me, dark eyes beyond warm.

"Now, what happened to make you think I'd changed my mind?"

Chapter Four
Cael

Cael went up the tree lightly, first pulling the dusky air about him like a cloak. He found the branch from which he had liberated Pretty Boots that afternoon, noting the claw marks in the tender wood, then followed the trail higher into the canopy, until he found the nest.

In the Land of the Flowers, willie wisps nested on the ground, for the trees would not have them. This tree was not so nice, or perhaps it was only ignorant of the strange new bird.

The nest reeked of willie wisp and fouled *jikinap*, its shape a tangled oval of bright bits of trash.

Cael sat astride a nearby branch and looked about him. Despite the season, leaves were thick around the nest, though they were brown, rather than the autumn colors of red or orange. The branches directly below the nest showed welts where droppings had irritated sensitive bark. These things were expectable.

What was peculiar were the shreds of *jikinap* in and around the nest.

Willie wisps were not mortal creatures, like a hound or a cat or a wolf. They were creatures of energy, and they fed on energy. Particularly, they fed on *jikinap*—magical energy—by *absorbing* it. There should be no crumbs left over, to drip onto and scar the branch below it.

Unless somebody was feeding it. Seeding the nest with *jikinap* so that the willie was certain to return to this spot, adjacent to what ought to have been—save for Pretty Boots—easy prey.

Cael frowned.

What if, he thought, the willie wisp had not been here so long, after all? What if it had arrived in the Changing Land *after* the Gate had closed?

Foolish wolf, he told himself. If the willie wisp has arrived since the closing of the Gate, the question to ask was, who had carried it? It was possible to cross from World to World without using a Gate or a Door, but it was dangerous, even for *ozali*. To bring anything extra, especially something as unpredictable, improbable, and useless as a willie wisp, courted disaster. What could possibly be worth such a risk?

The leaves above him rustled in a sudden breeze, which brought him the distinctive odor of willie wisp. Cael took a breath, stilling even his thoughts, waiting with a predator's terrible patience.

The leaves rustled again, and here was his prey—large for a willie wisp, which lent credence to the theory that someone was feeding it.

The creature dropped into its nest, sparking bluely as it began to feed.

It was of some importance to choose the correct Word. Too potent, and it might fire the tree. Too meager and annihilation might not be instantaneous. There was no need to cause unnecessary pain. Even to a willie wisp.

The willie continued to feed, oblivious to Cael's presence. He took a deep silent breath, and felt the Word form in his mouth. It tasted of ice and lightning. It would do.

Cael Spoke.

The Word left a glaze of frost on his lips. It enveloped the willie wisp in a brilliant ball of snow, contracting—and melting away, leaving the willie yet in its nest, scarcely disturbed at its meal.

Cael stared.

The willie wisp burped violet sparks.

Well, then.

Already, a second Word was forming, but before it was whole, the willie started, as if it had understood its danger, and bolted downward through the leaves.

Cael lunged after it, all the way down to the ground. It was dark enough now to hide him from anyone looking out from their house. But wolves have excellent night sight, and he was able to see the willie wisp bounding across the street toward a house with one bright-lit window open.

The willie hurtled toward that small opening, Cael a bare two steps behind. He was across the street, across the sidewalk, and the Word that had taken form was too large and too dire for the hunting of vermin.

The willie wisp put on a burst of speed, the window clearly its goal. The Word in Cael's mouth bore his tongue down, scraped the inside of his mouth. He must Speak, or choke.

He Spoke. The Word left soot on his tongue.

Ahead of him, one bounce short of the window, the willie wisp exploded into thick ruby streamers—and was gone.

Cael stopped on the sparse lawn, shivering a little. He tested the air, which smelled of ozone, salt, leaf mold—but not of willie wisp.

Satisfied—relieved—he turned to go.

A circle of white-hot *jikinap* blazed up around him, arcing higher than his head, blocking out the stars.

Chapter Five
Kate

Dinner done, we carried coffee mugs out to the deck overlooking the sea. I'd grown up calling it the "summer parlor," and its season was just about past. I shivered, and leaned against Borgan's chest for more than just the pleasure it gave me.

Oscar followed us out and sat with his nose poking between the pickets. Not a happy dog, Oscar, but he was being polite about it. Truth told, I didn't blame him for being a little antsy. For all his talk of reunions on the morrow, I'd expected Cael home sooner rather than later, and it was getting along to being *much* later.

"Reckon the willie didn't come back?" asked Borgan, reading the room.

"Maybe," I said, feeling something like actual worry, now that we were talking about it. "Willie wisps aren't exactly rocket scientists. Could've seen something else shiny—and easier to steal—and gone off after that." I sighed sharply. "What I don't like is that it keeps coming back to that tree—to Mrs. Newton. That says there's a nest."

"Which means it'll come back," Borgan said. "Only maybe not soon."

"Cael's got work tomorrow."

Cael *had* to work tomorrow, or Councilwoman Marcant would be in the town manager's office *that* quick, demanding he be fired. Getting fired from a town job in a town as small as Archers Beach meant you weren't likely to get another job—at least 'til summer came 'round again and you could pick up something at Fun Country, making pizza, or drawing ice cream, any of which would be too much work for too little pay. Wouldn't make him any different than the rest of the townies; that's the way staying alive worked in a resort town. It was just the sheer—*malice* of the thing that got stuck in my chest. Cael was good at his job; his boss liked him; the town liked him, the critters liked him. But Avis Marcant *didn't* like him—and it had nothing to do with the quality of his work.

"Figure to take a walk back up the hill?" Borgan asked.

I sighed, and finished my coffee.

"Sometimes, it's hard to know the right thing to do," I complained, and felt his laugh in my bones.

"Now, I've never found that."

"Liar."

Another rumble of laughter.

There aren't any fixed hours that go with being Guardian of the Land. Or for the Guardian of the Gulf of Maine, either. The fact was that willie wisps *didn't belong* in Archers Beach. Willie wisps didn't belong *any*where in the Changing Land, but the whole of the Changing Land wasn't my problem. Thank God.

Cael was more than capable of taking care of a willie wisp, him being both my oathsworn, like they say in the Land of the Flowers, and through me, bound to the Land known as Archers Beach.

However, Cael had not yet taken care of the willie, and Cael had other duties to fulfill.

And, if there was one stray willie in town, who's to say there weren't more?

I sighed again and straightened away from Borgan.

"Looks like the willie wisp stops here," I said. "Coming?"

"Why not?" Borgan said, taking the mug out of my hand. "Being honest, I'd like to get a look at that nest."

"All right, then." I turned—

Oscar howled.

The Land shouted inside my head, showing me wet red streamers raining down onto a scruffy lawn, the blinding glare of a working snapping into being—and something that felt like nothing—like an absence—a *specific* absence of Cael.

Oscar howled again, long and desolate.

I spun, took a step through the doorway into the house—

And another step, out onto Burdette Street, at the end of Mrs. Newton's driveway.

Chapter Six
Cael

"You caught the *dogcatcher*?"

Cael froze. He knew that voice. Avis Marcant, the councilwoman John had warned him about. But she was a woman of the Changing Land, all but blind to *jikinap*, as well as the wonders and horrors it produced. She ought not to have been able to *see* a willie wisp, much less make a pet of it. As to these burning bars that penned him—

"I do not know what a dogcatcher is." That voice he did *not* know, and having heard it once, he discovered in himself a desire never to hear it again. "But I *do* know power, and this—entity—possesses a significant amount. It may be that it will do."

Oh, power, was that it? Cael sighed and allowed the power to flow out of him, through the bottoms of his bare feet, into the Land, where it would be kept for him. It was unusual for someone to set such a trap in the Changing Land, where *jikinap* so often malfunctioned, or changed into something else under the influence of the Land's special attributes.

In Sempeki, such hunts were common, the acquisition of *jikinap* being vital to survival. Sempeki was the homeland of his liege, and himself. But there was something . . . odd about the circle of power confining him.

It didn't *feel* like Sempeki.

Cael stood patient, which was not easy. The trap was not large, and the bars were hot. Now that he was empty of all power, they were also *interested*, as *jikinap* is always interested, in filling empty vessels with itself.

"If you want him, take him," said Avis Marcant. "He's nothing but trouble; whole town'll be better off if he's someplace else."

"What I want," said the other in their jagged stony voice, "is the key to this place. What I have caught is not the key. The question I now ask is: Is this creature—valuable?"

"Valuable?" Avis Marcant repeated. "He's worthless."

"In that case, I do not want it."

"I mean, not worthless!" Avis Marcant cried. "Not to *you*. He's worthless to this town, like the old woman across the street. And you still owe me."

Cael took a careful breath, tasting *jikinap*, and wished he could see through the blazing bars that confined him.

"Creature!" the other voice said sharply. "What is your name?"

Cael felt his lips pull back from his teeth in a snarl. Did she think him as untutored as that? And, yet, why *not* give her a name? It might play to his advantage.

"My name," he said, "is Abraham Lincoln."

"No!" Avis Marcant began. "That's—"

"Be silent!" the rocky voice grated.

A gasp, and a brief silence, before more hard words.

"Abraham Lincoln, be bound where you stand."

The flames died on an instant, and Cael considered his captors. He stared into Avis Marcant's face for a long moment before turning to the other, who was—not of Sempeki, nor yet of the Changing Land. The face was vulpine, dark; the craggy grey body wrapt loosely in a long white shift, the eyes glittering white as quartz.

He was, Cael realized, looking at one of the Wise—never a good idea, and especially now, when the Gate between the Worlds had been closed—by order of the Wise—so that the Changing Land might die, for the crime of having offended them.

Cael settled his feet firmly against the grass, felt the Land's readiness.

"Abraham Lincoln, how did you dispatch the willie wisp?"

Cael moved his shoulders. "I got lucky."

"Give yourself up to me." The Wise One leaned forward, eyes glittering; the grey hand stretched out to him veined with marble.

Cael dared not pulled the Land's power into him. He was its protector, through his oath to his lady, and his own inclination. If the Wise One touched him while he was connected to the Land, she would touch—she would *foul*—Archers Beach. That he would not allow. Better to stand here, empty of all power, and take his chances with her temper.

"He lied to you," Avis Marcant gasped, either released from the Wise One's will or stronger than he believed her to be. "His name is Cael Wolfe, and he's the worst dogcatcher this town has ever had."

It was not his true-name, the one that he had been born to, in Sempeki, but it was his name in this Land, that defined who and what he was, here.

The quartz eyes sparkled. Cael felt the draw of another power on his soul. There was nothing he could do to resist her, empty as he stood. So far as weapons went, he had only one that he might wield without calling on any power save that which resided in him alone.

He closed his eyes, and opened his secret heart.

Chapter Seven
Kate

The Land showed me what was going on across the street, and a friendly breeze brought me voices; the words as clear as if I was right there beside them. The fright in the rock suit was definitely one of the Wise; I could see the power blazing around her like a halo. Avis Marcant—why—or how—Avis Marcant was in this, I couldn't fathom, except for the part where she was trying to get the fright to take Cael out of Archers Beach. *That* wasn't going to happen.

What worried me—a lot—was this talk of a *key*. A key to *this place*. Was the place Archers Beach, in particular? Or the whole of the Changing Land? Either way, it made no sense. The Wise had cut us out of the natural orbit of the Six Worlds. They'd shut the World Gate, and were perfectly willing to let us die—it being not yet proved that we *would* die. I had the idea that what was going to die were the rest of the Six Worlds, but nobody'd asked my opinion, and anyway what could one Guardian of a swath of Land in Maine that was the sole support of a rundown resort town, do against the Council of the Wise?

"He's lying," Avis Marcant yelled, which got my attention, sure enough. I took a breath, reached for the Land—

And saw Cael shiver against the night air, falling to four good feet and leaping away as a large grey wolf.

Avis Marcant screamed. The Wise One shouted a Word potent enough to peel paint. Cael kept on going, making for the trees at the bottom of the street.

I reached to the Land, which ought not to have registered as power on the Wise's radar, but guess what?

Lightning stitched the night, heading right toward me. I jumped sideways, toward the house, hoping the incoming was just your casual killing blade of power, rather than something that had been personally addressed to me.

I was lucky. The bolt passed through the place I'd been standing—and hit the Oldsmobile with a crackle and a BOOM!

The door slammed open at my back.

"Get in here! Now!" Angela Newton shouted.

I didn't wait to be told twice.

. . . .

CAEL RAN FOR THE TREES.

So far as he knew, they were *only* trees, nothing so terrible as the forest atop Heath Hill, the stronghold of his liege's grandmother and her consort. *Nothing* would get past *those* trees— possibly not Cael himself. The small grove he had chosen as his refuge in this moment of need would let him in, and—trees of the Land as they were, and owing fealty to Kate—they would protect him, man or wolf.

He loped across the asphalt. The undergrowth parted for him, and closed again as he slowed to a trot, stopping inside a small grassy clearing. Raising his nose, he tested the air, finding only the scents of an autumn wood. He heard no sound of pursuit, nor tasted *jikinap*. He might have had better information, if he touched the Land itself, but he felt himself safer as a simple wolf, innocent of power, fell or otherwise, and certainly innocent of the town's *dogcatcher*.

His hackles rose, and he felt a growl roughen his throat. Deliberately, he calmed his anger, stilled his thoughts. He was a wolf, simple and calm, hunting voles in the autumn forest, and nothing to draw the interest of one of the Great Wise Ones.

Around him, the trees waited. Cael shook his fur into order, and trotted across the clearing, disappearing between two pine trees, intent on finding the Heart of the wood.

• • • •

THE DOOR SLAMMED BEHIND me, and I sagged against the wall. I was in a narrow vestibule; the wall across from me was papered with a seashell print that had probably been bright and cheery, once. To my right was the closed door. Across from me was a wooden umbrella stand with three umbrellas waiting to be of service, above it was a rustic wooden wall shelf, a set of keys hanging on one of the three iron hooks beneath a cheery stenciled Welcome Home!

To my left—was Angela Newton, standing in the doorway that must open into the rest of the house. She was wearing jeans and a sweatshirt, and clutching a pudgy grey-and-white cat to her chest.

"Are you all right?" she asked.

"I'm fine. I appreciate you letting me in. Things were getting a little hot out there."

"That woman!" Mrs. Newton exploded. "She's a menace, and her tame real estate agent, too! If she thinks I'm going to sell her this house—well, I *told* her I wouldn't! Why would I sell it? It's my home! My husband and I lived here all the years we were married, our kids grew up here—it's paid off! I grew up in this town! Where would I *go*, if I sold this house?"

"Won't take no for an answer?" I asked, easing away from the wall and sending a sharp glance at the door to be certain it was locked. It was, but there was only so much brass and wood could stand against, if Rocky the Wise decided she wanted in.

I extended a request to the Land, and felt living green energy wrap itself around the door frame, and weave across the door itself, which was something a little better in the way of protection.

"It's completely ridiculous! I told her no, that should've been the end of it! Then she produces this realtor, ready to write me a *blank check* and laughing at me when I said I wouldn't sell at any price. And now—loud music at all hours, fireworks after curfew—they're trying to force me out, I know that, and I know they'll find someway to make it worse, if I talk to the police, so I haven't, but if they're going to start threatening other people, to somehow make it my fault that these dreadful things are happening . . . ."

Suddenly, she began to cry, her face turned away as if she was ashamed that I was seeing it.

I moved forward, and the cat in her arms—Pretty Boots, it must be—glared at me. I stopped, and the Land tugged on my sleeve. Not literally, but—just say the Land wanted my attention.

Ripples of power reached me—nothing at all like the usual feel of the Land, though there was something . . . tantalizingly familiar there. I queried, and got the Land's assurance that Avis and Rocky weren't on the lawn across the street anymore, which was only a limited comfort.

I asked about Cael, which was greeted with a sense of puzzlement before I got a glimpse of a big grey wolf moving quiet between trees. Nearby, that was the sense I got, and then the exact taste of the little spinney at the intersection of Burdette Street and Foote flooded my mouth.

All right, that was good. Wolf in the wood, no problem. Unless Rocky had gone after him, in which case I didn't like his chances. Not that Cael was without resources, but he wasn't drawing on the Land. I'd almost been killed by one of the Wise while I'd been standing in a power center in my own Land. I don't know what the Wise draw on, but there doesn't seem to be any limit to it.

The Land did the metaphysical equivalent of tugging on my sleeve again, and my senses were suddenly flooded with green determination, and a lingering taste of vanilla. The little wood on Foote Street, that was again, showing me its muscles.

"What should I do?" Mrs. Newton asked me, still clutching Pretty Boots to her chest.

I sighed and stepped toward her.

"First, you need to tell me who you are, and how long this Door's been here."

Chapter Eight
Cael

The Heart of the wood was a white oak tree. Cael the wolf paced toward it, drawn by the scent of vanilla and the cool sense of peace.

The tree stood on a knoll, uncrowded by lesser trees, strong pale branches arching out and up. Cael paused at the foot of the small rise, gazing up to leaves turned golden with September, light brown acorns clustered tight among them.

It was a worthy hiding place, and Cael doubted that either the Wise or Avis Marcant would seek him here.

Which only left the question of his next move. Kate would have heard the Wise One's assault and would have rushed to the defense of her Land. *That* was the cloth from which his lady was cut, and in his secret heart, he would have her no different. A wolf could love such a liege, even as he feared for her safety.

Nor was she without allies. Her consort, the sea lord, was not to be dismissed; nor those others who served the Land of which she was Guardian. All of those would have heard the racket of the Wise One's assault, and would be standing at the centers of their own small powers, ready to defend.

He ought to make his way to Kate's side, and assist in her defense of the Land. The only question remained was—ought he to go as wolf or man?

"*Another* one?" demanded a voice that was both pleasing and annoyed.

Cael lowered his gaze from the tree's proud branches, to find a sturdy figure clothed in a grey hoodie over a pair of grey sweatpants standing beside the ash-grey bole. The hood was thrust back, revealing short white hair, and a round, olive-toned face. Her eyebrows were umber, and her eyes a deep and glittering gold. She stood with her hands on her hips, and the sense that Cael caught from her was not . . . entirely . . . peaceful.

"I guess *you* got lost in the wind, too?"

Cael sat down and considered her. She stamped a bare foot against the knoll's short grass.

"Answer me! I, the White Lady of the Wood, command you!"

Disconnected from the Land as he was, still Cael felt the force of that command, as it flowed past him, the wolf disinterested in the lady's display of dominance.

She raised her eyebrows.

"This is a small holding," she said, her voice somewhat more moderate. "I already have one wolf to hold; I can't keep two. Go away. The wind has died; you can find your way home."

Another wolf? Who had been lost in the wind? The Wind Between the Worlds, would that be, that had been realigned as part of Prince Aesgyr's rebellion against the Wise? How long had this other wolf been here? Why? And did this have anything to do with the Wise One and the willie wisp?

These were, Cael thought, weighty questions for a wolf. He therefore opened his secret heart.

The White Lady glared at him.

"I said *go away*, not change forms."

"My apologies, Lady, but I belong to this Land."

Her glare softened momentarily, and Cael felt her query the Land. An affirmative was returned, somewhat aggrieved, which Cael also felt.

"You're not *trenvay*," she stated, which was both correct—and not correct.

"I am oathsworn to Kate Archer. I serve the Land through that bond."

"I can see you, and I can sense you, but the Land isn't nourishing you," she said, and tipped her head. "It's a little upset about that."

"I regret," Cael said. He could feel the Land's distress, and longed to reach out to it, to find where was his liege and her condition.

"What are you doing in my wood?"

"Hiding, Lady."

Her eyebrows rose.

"Hiding from what?"

"Enemies of the Land, and of the Guardian."

She stiffened.

"You brought danger to my wood?"

"I think not, Lady. I withdrew myself from the Land, as you see, and assumed my other form, which is merely a part of my nature. Those enemies, they seek power; they follow power. As a wolf, and now as a man, I have no power."

"Fine. Go away. I don't want you here."

She was the goddess of the oak, protector of the grove, and surely she had every right to order him gone. Only, there was one other thing.

Cael rose, and bowed.

"May I," he murmured delicately, "speak with the wolf you hold here?"

• • • •

"DOOR?" ANGELA NEWTON stared at me, shoulders tightening, her grip on Pretty Boots going even tighter. "The front door's been here as long as the house. As to who I am—I ought to be asking who *you* are!"

Fair enough.

"I'm Kate Archer. I own the carousel down in Fun Country."

Amazingly, she relaxed somewhat.

"I read about you in the paper," she said. "You made sure the park's going to stay in town."

That . . . was something of a stretch, but I wasn't going to argue about it this minute. Instead, I smiled and nodded, touched the Land, and extended a tiny curl of *jikinap*, seeking an answering flicker of power from Angela Newton.

There was no reaction, except a slight feeling of gentle care from the Land. Angela Newton was exactly as she presented—an old woman of mundane heritage, not a shred of other worlds or magic about her.

In the interest of completion, I examined Pretty Boots, who was, in her turn, just a cat, insofar as a cat can be "just."

"But—what door?" Angela Newton asked me.

The Door. Right. I'd felt it the instant I was inside the house, and the longer I stood here in the hall, the more uncomfortable I was getting. Private Doors between one or another of the Six Worlds shouldn't exist, according to the Wise, who liked to keep track of commerce between the Worlds, or maybe I mean smuggling. Despite that, such things *do* exist, but usually, they're warded and very quiet.

This Door was noisy, to the point that it was making my teeth itch.

"I'm thinking that I know what interest this real estate agent of Avis' has in your property," I told Angela Newton. "Mind if I take a look in your basement?"

She stared at me, then nodded. "All right. Is it something that can be removed? If I give it to them, will they *stop* and just—leave us alone?"

"It's a little technical," I told her. "I'll know more after I see how it's been installed."

Her forehead wrinkled a little at that, and her grip on Pretty Boots must have increased; the cat wriggled imperiously, and the woman bent to put her down.

Straightening, she waved a hand at me, turning toward the doorway behind her.

"Basement door's in the kitchen," she said. "I'll show you. And you'll want a flashlight."

· · · ·

HEAD ON FRONT PAWS, the wolf lay at the center of a fairy ring. Peaceful humors laced the breeze, and Cael caught the tang of forgetting, and something else, far more concerning.

He turned to the White Lady.

"Why did you imprison this wolf?"

She drew herself up, haughty goddess, and looked down her nose at him.

"She was wounded and confused when she came into my wood. I have the deer and the small lives to protect! I couldn't risk them, so I put her to heal."

That was very much the solution of a goddess, Cael thought. To heal the wounded—that would be at her core, as would the necessity to protect those who resided in her honor. To do both, while endangering neither would be a challenge, and the solution doomed to be uneven.

"Is she healed?" he asked.

The goddess looked troubled.

"In her body, yes. In her mind? I fear not. I note disturbing dreams and confusing thoughts. My best wisdom was to allow sleep to do its work."

"It is my intention to wake her," Cael said, "and to take her away from this wood." That would be true, even if the wolf were only a wolf, which, as he was becoming increasingly convinced, was not the case.

"You're worried," the White Lady said. "Have I done harm?"

It was never wise to criticize a goddess. Yet, what if another such fell to her hand? Her concern carried the scent of truth; she wished to learn better, and it was his to teach her.

"It's in my mind that this wolf is another such as myself," he said slowly. "Which is to say, she has two natures, and is not *only* a wolf. This duality of nature demands some care. If I am a man too long, I risk starving my wolf, and cutting myself off from the wisdoms inherent in that nature. If I am a wolf too long—"

"You may forget how to be a man," the White Lady interrupted. "In fact, I may have doomed her to a single nature." She turned to look at him. "How will I heal this?"

"First, allow me to wake and speak with her. It may be that not . . . much harm has been done. How long has she been here?"

The goddess blinked, and Cael bit his lip. What was time, after all, to a goddess?

"She came two days after Lammas," she said, surprisingly.

That . . . was not very long at all, then, Cael thought. Assuming that it had been Lammas just past that the goddess remembered.

"If that is so," he said carefully, "then she may have escaped grievous harm. May I enter and speak with her?"

"Yes. Wake her and take her away. I give you leave."

She moved her hand, and the sweet humors of the air dissipated, even as the goddess herself faded away.

Cael turned to look at the wolf in the ring, who stretched, and yawned, and opened eyes as green as grass.

• • • •

"ROAD'S CLOSED? WHAT for?" asked the man in the red pickup truck.

Borgan gave him a friendly smile, and leaned close to the side window, shaking a little sea-calm off his fingertips.

"Got a little bit of a situation around Miz Marcant's house," he murmured, nice and easy. "Rescue and cops're on the way."

The sea-calm did its work, and the driver didn't say that the cops were less than five minutes away and the Rescue even closer, nor even ask was Miz Marcant all right. Instead, he nodded, and smiled at Oscar, sitting neatly at the curb.

"Right, then," he said, "I'll go 'round. Nice dog you got there."

"The best," Borgan said, stepping back, and giving a brisk wave. "Off you go, now."

Chapter Nine
Kate

It was a Door all right.

I could see the crisped, twisted remains of what must have once been significant wards, scattered across the stone floor.

Even standing back near the stairs, I could hear a hard wind howling—the Wind that Blew Between the Worlds, and nothing to play with, even on a good day. Every so often a gust would hit the Door and it would jump.

Not what you'd call a safe condition.

I would like it to be on record that I *did not* open the Door, just to see what was on the other side. I didn't even get close enough to put my hand against it, though I won't say I wasn't tempted.

There was no question in my mind that the Door was what Rocky was after, whether to ward it or open it was still an open question, though whichever it was, I was betting it wouldn't be good for this, my Land.

I looked around again at the burnt and busted wards, and winced. That had not been a trivial expenditure of *jikinap*. I didn't even want to think about how much power it was going to take to reweave and reinforce those so the Door was hidden again.

"One thing at a time, Kate," I muttered, and went back upstairs.

• • • •

THE WOLF WAS ALMOST dainty, brown coat shot with gold, ears well-set, tail held at neutral. Waiting.

Cael inclined his head.

"I am Cael, called the Wolf, oathsworn to Lady Aeronymous, who is also Kate Archer, Guardian of this Land. I bid you stand forth, and give an accounting."

The wolf blinked, lazily, and glanced over her shoulder at the ring and the wood beyond.

"The White Lady releases you," Cael said. "She has small lives, and gentle, to protect. Again, I bid you stand forth."

The moment stretched; even the wind was silent. If he asked a third time, she would be compelled, and he did not—

The air moved in a bright swirl and before him stood a woman of Sempeki, brown hair striped with gold and drawn back from a long-nosed face dominated by a pair of grass green eyes.

"I am Assa, called the Huntress. I am under geas to neutralize Corraiga the Wise, a known villain. I had tracked her to the threshold of the Changing Land before the Wind roared between the Worlds, and spun us apart. I was battered, burned, and, I fear, broken, before I found myself in the White Lady's grove, where I could scarcely recall my own name."

She lifted her chin and met his eyes firmly.

"I heard what you said to her, but truly, she has done more good than ill. I have lost the scent, though, and must begin again. I only hope that Corraiga has done no great mischief in the time since we were separated."

"I believe I know where this Wise One is," Cael said, and touched the Land, lightly.

An image appeared in the air before them, the white shift worn over the craggy body, the quartz-white eyes . . .

"Yes! That is Corraiga the Wise. Where—"

At that moment, the Land screamed; the image of the Wise One replaced with another, more horrific, and the air was filled with ice.

Cael snatched Assa's hand and ran.

• • • •

"WELL, IT WAS A GOOD install, once upon a time," I told Angela Newton, as I put the flashlight back on the kitchen counter. "It's taken a beating, though. I can call in a technician, if you want; fix it up; so nobody knows it's there, like it used to be."

"How do they—the realtor?—how does he know it's there now? Special instrumentation?"

I nodded. "Like that. I'm betting she was just looking to see what she could find, like those folks with their metal detectors, down on the beach—and yours just popped up, by chance."

She looked downtrodden.

"My bad luck."

"Not necessarily. Now you know it's got to be fixed. And I know how to get it fixed." Maybe.

"How much will that cost?" she asked, and it was on the edge of my tongue to tell her to wait until I'd found the right tech, when the house shook under the force of a blow from above. The Land showed me the roof, and a branch, and I didn't wait for anything else.

"The tree!" I yelled, grabbing the woman's arm and pulling her out of her chair. "Go, go! Out the back door!"

"Bootsy!" Angela Newton cried, twisting away from me with unexpected strength. She rushed down the hall. I jumped for the back door, wrenched it open—and here she came back again, at a dead run, the cat folded against her chest.

She flew down the back stairs, me right on her heels, hitting the ground, and hearing the Land wail just as I braked hard, staring into Avis Marcant's grim and determined face, over the barrel of a shotgun.

I reached for the Land. Avis Marcant yelled, which was reasonable, since she was suddenly knee-deep in dirt. Her finger tightened on the trigger—but the gun was no longer a gun; it was a piece of driftwood, still wet from the ocean.

Give her credit, she yelled again, and made a good-faith effort to bean me with it, only I ducked inside her swing, and she jerked back, the driftwood spinning out of her grip as she fell.

"You will give me the key!" Rocky snarled nearby, and I turned, seeing her approaching Mrs. Newton, *jikinap* crackling, one tendril whipping around to strike the woman on the shoulder.

She cried out in pain, and that right there was too much for Pretty Boots, who twisted out of her arms, and threw herself, claws out, at Rocky's face.

No question, it was a valiant effort, and Bootsy had a hero's heart—but the face was granite, the eyes were quartz, and Rocky was wroth. A swing, a connect, a sharp sound, like twigs snapping, and Bootsy was flying, then falling, limp as a broken flower, disappearing among the dropped leaves littering the grass.

Mrs. Newton screamed, and leapt forward, hands out, fingers curled—and was caught up by none other than Cael the Wolf, who spun away with her in his arms, while a woman I'd never seen before stepped close to Rocky, seized her wrists and uttered a Word.

Time stopped.

When it started again, Rocky was immobile in the stranger's grip, her *jikinap* a whirling ball of vile and sullen lightnings, spinning and spitting above their heads.

I frowned. In the usual way of things, in a duel between users of *jikinap*, the loser's power was forfeit to the winner. Only, this winner didn't seem all that eager to claim her prize.

"Coward!" Rocky grated. "Are you afraid of power?"

"I am afraid of *your* power," the victor answered, and the Land showed me what she was spending to keep that loathsome ball at bay, even as she held Rocky in thrall.

"Assa, what would you?" Cael called.

"Give me a task to which I may release it! Quickly!"

I jumped to her side.

"Got just the thing!" I said, and met the bright green gaze she bent on me. "There's a Door that needs to be warded."

She gave me the grimmest smile I've ever seen on a woman's face, and the most satisfied one, too.

"Help me," she said.

"First thing is clean it," I said, reaching to the Land, which responded with surprising ferocity.

"Right," I said, and nodded at Assa.

"Give it to me," I said.

It was jagged, actively malevolent, and there was—so much. For a heartbeat, I questioned my plan, but it was already too late. Rocky's *jikinap* flowed through me, into the Land, and, following my thought, wrapped 'round the noisy door.

I staggered, and Assa caught me with a firm hand under my arm.

"Have to build real wards, later," I managed. "But that'll do for now."

I looked around.

"Where's Rocky?"

Assa's eyebrows twitched, and then she laughed, sweet as merrybells. "Rocky? I see. Her true name was Corraiga the Wise. She was unmade, of course, when you reft her of her power."

Of course, I thought, and couldn't quite find it in me to shed a tear.

Chapter Ten

Kate

It was done quick enough, after that.

Cael helped Mrs. Newton find where Bootsy had landed, and knelt with her while she cried. I felt the flicker, so faint, and Cael did, too. A second later, I felt the draw on the Land, then Mrs. Newton was crying aloud, "Bootsy! You're alive!"

Around about then, the cops showed up, and the Rescue; Borgan and Oscar, too. Borgan busied himself helping Avis Marcant get up onto her feet, and I felt a particular salty breeze pass by my ear.

Rescue gave all of us a rough-and-ready examination, and all of us, except Avis Marcant, refused transport to the hospital.

"It was Cael Wolfe who saved us!" I heard her say, as she was bundled up in a blanket and led to the ambulance.

"That's right, Avis," I heard the EMT answer, and recognized him for Jerry, one of the *trenvay* from the wetlands. "He's a good man, our Cael."

"None better," she said fervently. "And I'm going to tell the mayor so!"

I turned to look at Borgan about then, and Borgan looked at me, his face too innocent.

"What happens," I asked, "when she comes to herself?"

"Might not come back all the way," he said comfortably. "Little bit o'sea change never hurt nobody."

"Borgan—"

"So," Mrs. Newton interrupted, standing before us with Bootsy in her arms. "You'll be getting that tech for me, so this never happens again?"

I blinked, then, prompted by the Land, looked over to the side, where Cael and Assa Huntress were standing, heads together. I made a request, and heard her say, " . . . not back to Sempeki. I wish—an honorable service."

"Just a sec," I said to Mrs. Newton. "Comes to me that Assa used to do that kind of work."

I stepped over to the private conference.

"Excuse me," I said, "I couldn't help but overhear. Might be I could provide an honorable service."

Assa turned to me, green eyes wide.

"I am listening."

"Right. The elder and her cat are valiant and fierce in their protection of each other. But there are no servants, no children, no knights. And there is that Door in the basement, which is probably going to need a close eye kept on it for some time."

"You propose that I stay here to serve the elders, and to guard the Door."

"That's it. Unless that's not honorable enough for you."

"You will need to take an oath of fealty, to my lady, the Guardian of this Land," Cael said from beside her, and I saw Assa catch her breath as she realized what that would mean. That she would no longer be of Sempeki, but sworn and bound to the Changing Land.

The Land brought me the moment she made her decision, and an echo of the gladness that bloomed in her heart.

She dropped to one knee, and held out her hands, palms up. I put my hands over hers.

"I, Assa, do swear that I will keep faith with the Guardian and the Land and never cause either harm. I will defend them and reverence them, and in all things obey them. This I swear upon my life."

The oath hit the Land with a *crack*! I felt power rise up, through me, through her, binding us, liege and oathsworn.

Assa gasped, and swayed on her knees. Cael stepped forward to catch her shoulders and help her stand.

"Done," he said, "and done well. Finish it, now."

"Yes," she said softly, and shook herself, flashing me a grin as she stood forward.

"Yes, Kate," she said, loud enough to be heard across the yard. "How good of you to remember! I still do that sort of work."

I brought her over for introductions, reaching down to the Land as I made them.

"Pleased to meet you," Mrs. Newton said, and Bootsy deigned to deliver a cat-smile.

"I am pleased to meet you, too, Grandmother," Assa said softly. "I will stay and be certain that you are left in peace."

"Course you will," Mrs. Newton said. "My own granddaughter? There's plenty room, and Bootsy will be glad of extra company." She paused and slanted a glance into Assa's face.

"Can you climb trees?"

"Grandmother," Assa said seriously, "I can."

"Good," said Mrs. Newton. "Then we're set. Come on in now, and I'll show you your room."

Assa followed her into the house, and I felt the ripple of the whisper she sent through the Land, for Cael's ears alone, and smiled.

Cael and Oscar left, heading for home; tomorrow was a work day, after all. Borgan and I walked out front to look at the damage that had been done by the falling tree.

"Looks like it's just that one branch come down," Borgan said. "She'll need a tree service, though."

"Or maybe not," I said, taking his hand, as we turned back down the street. "I'm thinking Assa has pertinent skills there, too."

He laughed quietly. "Might, at that."

About the Author

M aine author Sharon Lee is known for her SF and fantasy novels and stories, especially the Liaden Universe® series co-authored with her late husband, Steve Miller, which spans nearly thirty novels and many short works, transporting readers to a universe where diplomacy, trade, and traditions intertwine.

Her work is known for complex characters and intricate plotlines as she explores themes of loyalty, friendship, love, and the balance between tradition and progress.

Lee's passion for storytelling showed at an early age as she crafted imaginative tales for her own amusement. She met in a college writing course her future writing partner, cat friend, and husband Steve Miller; they began collaborating in her universes shortly before joining households.

Sharon has also penned several solo novels, including *Barnburner* and *Gunshy*, cozy mysteries, and fantasy trilogy *Carousel Tides*, *Carousel Sun*, and *Carousel Seas*, all set in her adopted state of Maine.

Lee's accolades include NESFA's Skylark Award and the Prism Award.

Sharon Lee lives in Maine with several very loud muses in the form of Maine Coon cats.

Novels by Sharon Lee & Steve Miller

The **Liaden Universe®:** Agent of Change * Conflict of Honors * Carpe Diem * Plan B * Local Custom * Scout's Progress * I Dare * Balance of Trade * Crystal Soldier * Crystal Dragon * Fledgling * Saltation * Mouse and Dragon * Ghost Ship * Dragon Ship * Necessity's Child * Trade Secret * Dragon in Exile * Alliance of Equals * The Gathering Edge * Neogenesis * Accepting the Lance * Trader's Leap * Fair Trade * Salvage Right * Ribbon Dance * Diviner's Bow

Omnibus Editions: The Dragon Variation * The Agent Gambit * Korval's Game * The Crystal Variation

Story Collections: A Liaden Universe® Constellation: Volume 1 * A Liaden Universe Constellation®: Volume 2 * A Liaden Universe® Constellation: Volume 3 * A Liaden Universe® Constellation: Volume 4 * A Liaden Universe Constellation®: Volume 5

The Fey Duology: Duainfey * Longeye

Gem ser'Edreth: The Tomorrow Log

Novels by Sharon Lee

The Carousel Trilogy: Carousel Tides * Carousel Sun * Carousel Seas

Jennifer Pierce Maine Mysteries: Barnburner * Gunshy

Pinbeam Books Publications

Sharon Lee and Steve Miller's indie publishing arm

Adventures in the Liaden Universe®: Two Tales of Korval *
Fellow Travelers * Duty Bound * Certain Symmetry * Trading
in Futures * Changeling * Loose Cannon * Shadows and Shades *
Quiet Knives * With Stars Underfoot * Necessary Evils * Allies *
Dragon Tide * Eidolon * Misfits * Halfling Moon * Skyblaze *
Courier Run * Legacy Systems * Moon's Honor * Technical Details
* Sleeping with the Enemy * Change Management * Due Diligence
* Cultivar * Heirs to Trouble * Degrees of Separation * Fortune's
Favor * Shout of Honor * The Gate that Locks the Tree * Ambient
Conditions * Change State * Bad Actors * Bread Alone * From
Every Storm

Splinter Universe Presents: Splinter Universe Presents:
Volume One * The Wrong Lance

By Sharon Lee: Variations Three * Endeavors of Will * The
Day they Brought the Bears to Belfast * Surfside * The Gift of
Magic * Spell Bound * Writing Neep * Doors into Change *
Sea Wrack and Changewind

By Steve Miller: Chariot to the Stars * TimeRags II

By Sharon Lee and Steve Miller: Calamity's Child * The Cat's
Job * Master Walk * Quiet Magic * The Naming of Kinzel *
Reflections on Tinsori Light * Double Vision

Thank You

Thank you for your support of my work.
                                            —Sharon Lee

www.ingramcontent.com/pod-product-compliance
Lightning Source LLC
Chambersburg PA
CBHW020108180626
46812CB00006B/2522